Traci Douglass is a *USA TODAY* bestselling author of contemporary and paranormal romance. Her stories feature sizzling heroes full of dark humour, quick wit and major attitude, and heroines who are smart, tenacious and always give as good as they get. She holds an MFA in Writing Popular Fiction from Seton Hill University, and she loves animals, chocolate, coffee, hot British actors and sarcasm— not necessarily in that order.

Also by Traci Douglass

One Night with the Army Doc

Discover more at millsandboon.co.uk.

FINDING HER FOREVER FAMILY

TRACI DOUGLASS

MILLS & BOON

First published in Great Britain 2019
by Mills & Boon, an imprint of HarperCollins*Publishers*
1 London Bridge Street, London, SE1 9GF

Large Print edition 2019

© 2019 Traci Douglass

ISBN: 978-0-263-07859-6

MIX
Paper from
responsible sources
FSC **FSC C007454**
www.fsc.org

This book is produced from independently certified FSC™ paper to ensure responsible forest management. For more information visit www.harpercollins.co.uk/green.

Printed and bound in Great Britain
by CPI Group (UK) Ltd, Croydon, CR0 4YY

To my wonderful editors,
Sheila Hodgson and Charlotte Ellis,
who helped me craft this story
into something worth reading.

To Laura McCallen, for finding me in
a flurry of entries and working with me
until her departure.

To my agent, Dawn Dowdle,
who shepherded me through the process
on these first two books.

To my critique partner, Coleen Burright,
the best beta reader in the world.

To my wonderful tribe in the SHU
Writing Popular Fiction Program
and my Secret Keepers, who are all
a beacon of light in the storm.

To my family, for always believing in me.

And, last but not least…
To my readers, who make all of this
possible. THANK YOU. I wouldn't get
to do what I love without all of you!
♥

CHAPTER ONE

"Where's the server?" ER Trauma Nurse Wendy Smith asked as she and her sister-in-law, Aiyana, grabbed a table at the Snaggle Tooth. The pub was all but empty, and she was disappointed to find no trace of an employee anywhere.

"Welcome!" a guy finally shouted from the kitchen doorway, eyeing Aiyana's enormous belly with trepidation. "Be with you in a second."

Her sister-in-law, besides being married to Wendy's oldest brother, Ned, was also thirty-seven weeks pregnant with twins. Wendy felt sorry for her, and a bit envious, to be honest.

Not that she'd share those feelings with anyone.

Having children of her own wasn't in the cards.

It had been Aiyana's idea to eat a late lunch

at the pub today and against Wendy's better judgment she'd said yes. The place held special memories for her sister-in-law. It was where she and Ned had gone on their first date. The pub was also where Wendy's friend and boss, Dr. Jake Ryder, had taken his new wife, Dr. Molly Flynn, after their first date. Seemed the place was crawling with love bugs. Wendy did her best not to itch.

But at least the food was good. And when a hungry pregnant woman suggested the place that served her favorite comfort meal, you didn't argue.

Aiyana picked up a menu off the scarred wooden tabletop, then shifted in her seat, trying to get comfortable. At near full-term, however, it wasn't happening.

"Need help?" Wendy asked.

"What I need is a crowbar." Seemed the only part of her usually effervescent sister-in-law that functioned properly these days was her appetite. Everything else had gone wonky because of sleep deprivation and abundant hormones.

"How about we split the salmon nachos?"

Wendy suggested, perusing her menu. "Looks like they have your favorite Peanut Butter Brownie Surprise for dessert too. Anything else?"

"A side of Pitocin." Aiyana winced and rubbed her lower back. "All the books I read made having a baby sound like a breeze. This is not my idea of fun."

Wendy hailed the waiter to place their order, then settled back in the booth. "Have you and Ned decided on names?"

Aiyana shook her head as the server brought them water. "We've been busy."

True. In addition to becoming a new dad soon, Ned was learning the ropes to take over the family mechanic shop from their father. Her other two brothers, Jim and Mike, were also busy, shouldering the extra duties Ned had left behind when he'd become the manager. Wendy helped out there when she could, despite her busy schedule at Anchorage Mercy, figuring it was the least she could do since they'd raised her after Mom had died.

Wendy had been just ten when it had happened, but she remembered it like yesterday.

She sighed. Her thirtieth birthday was looming, and she'd begun to hear the ticktock of her biological clock louder than ever, no matter how improbable.

But getting pregnant, for her, would be a huge disaster, even if she did secretly want a baby of her own. Life was hard when you could be a walking genetic time bomb. Huntington's disease had taken everything from her poor mother by the end of her too-short life. She'd been unable to walk, talk, swallow. She'd died a shell of the vibrant woman she'd once been.

The thought of leaving behind a husband and children was too devastating to consider.

So it was best not to go down that route at all.

Wendy had been tested, of course, at age eighteen, just as her brothers had been before her. But they'd all been in serious relationships at the time they'd gotten their results, so it seemed more urgent for them to find out. She hadn't been seeing anyone when she'd had her testing. In fact, she'd been ready to head off to college and begin her nursing career. With all that pressure, the last thing she'd wanted was a Huntington's positive result looming over her head too. She'd always figured there'd be plenty of time to find out later. Then, as the years had passed, and her life had moved on, the time had never seemed right.

Her brothers had all been negative for the gene mutation that caused Huntington's disease. There was a fifty-fifty shot of inheriting. Being the last out of four siblings…well, Wendy knew the odds weren't in her favor. It would've been a miracle if she was negative too, and when it came to her own mortality she wasn't the betting type. So, twelve years on, she'd never requested her results, never wanted to know, never wanted to play Russian roulette with her own life. Just the thought of spending the rest of her days like a dead woman walking, terrified of every twitch or stumble, thinking the end was near, was terrifying.

Instead, she'd gone in the opposite direction, living life to the fullest. All to conceal the shame and fear of possibly being afflicted with an incurable disease. Maybe some people took that as running away from her problems or being a coward. Wendy didn't care. Let those people walk a mile in her shoes.

No sense pretending a happily-ever-after was in her future.

Not when those you cared for could be ripped away from you at any time.

Love was a definite no-go for Wendy. No risk. No reward. No problem.

Across from her, Aiyana inhaled deeply and slowly, her hands sliding across the table, fingers splayed in an effort to control her breathing, her lung capacity compromised by the twins shoving up against them.

"You should probably get on that whole naming thing," Wendy said, raising a brow. "Looks like you don't have much longer to go."

The server interrupted them with a platter of hot nachos and two plates.

Wendy grabbed a handful of chips and put them on her plate, knowing if she didn't act now Aiyana would devour the food and she'd never get any.

Their waiter's gaze darted from her sister-in-law's belly to Wendy's little pile of nachos then back again. "Did you want ice cream with the dessert, ma'am?"

"Two scoops, please," Aiyana said.

The server departed, and Wendy flicked open her napkin. "That's a lot of food."

"What difference does it make? I'm already as big as a house." Aiyana's bottom lip trembled, and her eyes sparkled with tears. Wendy felt awful. She'd not meant it that way. "But I'm always hungry and Ned's working overtime to make up for when he'll be off after the babies are born and I haven't found another person to cover for me at the souvenir shop and…" Aiyana flinched and grabbed her belly, bending over and inhaling sharply. "Braxton Hicks contractions."

After a moment, her sister-in-law relaxed and dug into the platter of nachos. Within minutes, as predicted, all the food was gone. She chugged down her water then banged the glass on the tabletop like a Viking. The server left a pitcher of water on the table.

"Obviously we need names for the birth certificates," Aiyana said, chewing suspiciously.

Wendy looked at her own plate to find the rest of her nachos gone too. "Hey!"

A guilty look crossed her pretty face. "Sorry."

Thankfully, the waiter soon came to the rescue, bringing the piping-hot Peanut Butter Brownie Surprise and an extra fork.

Her sister-in-law deftly changed subjects, speaking around a mouthful of chocolate and ice cream. "Carmen says we'll give it five more days. Then we'll reassess."

Carmen Sanchez was her sister-in-law's certified nurse midwife. With a master's degree in nursing, she was sort of like an obstetrician and a midwife combined, except she couldn't perform surgery. If Aiyana did end up needing a C-section they'd have to use the OB on call at Anchorage Mercy at the time of delivery.

From years of working in the ER, Wendy knew *that* could be a crapshoot. Thankfully, Aiyana's pregnancy had gone without a hitch thus far, so she could stay with her midwife, but the ever-present threat of preeclampsia and obstetric cholestasis meant the OB/GYN department was ready at all times, just in case.

"Well, you've got my number on speed dial," Wendy said. "And you know I'll show up anytime, anywhere, whenever these kids decide to be born."

Aiyana looked up from her dessert, her cheeks

persistently rosy this late in pregnancy. "Thank you."

"You're welcome." Wendy smiled. "Someone's got to keep my brother in line while you're in labor, right?"

"Right." Laughing, Aiyana eased out of the booth. "Need to use the restroom. Be right back."

She waddled away, and Wendy's throat constricted with unexpected tears.

She'd not expected to be so emotional over the impending delivery of the twins. Everything was about to change. Ned and Aiyana would have new responsibilities, new obligations, new lives to embark on. While she would stay stuck inside her self-imposed bubble, safe and protected and happy.

And I am happy, right?

Sure, she'd made sacrifices because of a potential medical diagnosis. But Wendy had been inconsolable for weeks after her mom's passing. Her universe had imploded and when her world had re-formed, she'd been different—more guarded, more responsible, less carefree and reliant on others.

Two decades had passed, but not much had changed.

Maybe her social life had suffered lately because she was so busy. Didn't matter. She wasn't looking for a relationship. Which was good because it was hard to meet men when you worked eighty-plus hours a week.

These days she had fun, dated, got involved with guys who were looking for a good time, not a long-term relationship, and kept what was left of her battered heart out of the equation.

And so what if, sometimes, those niggles of yearning—the ones that whispered how wonderful it might be to have a baby and family of her own—became too persistent? She'd soon have her newborn niece and nephew to satisfy that craving.

Plus, now there was Sam at work to keep her company.

A friend who was a youth counselor at Anchorage Mercy had been going on vacation, and had asked Wendy if she'd be willing to help out with one of the kids she was treating who'd recently lost her mother. It was a no-brainer, given Wendy's past and the fact she'd trained to volunteer helping at-risk youth at the hospital, which meant she'd already been screened and vetted. Sam was twelve and full of snark, reminding Wendy of herself at that age. Sam's father also worked at the hospital, but, with her busy schedule, Wendy hadn't had a chance to meet him yet. Plus, since she'd only be covering for a short time, it hadn't seemed like a top priority.

Over her few visits with Sam, though, Wendy had come to enjoy them and looked forward to those late-lunch chats.

Sam was like the kid sister Wendy had never had.

The sound of clattering dishes drew her attention to the afternoon sunshine filtering through the pub windows, flashing across tabletops and sparkling through rows of glasses and bottles waiting for customers behind the bar. The air smelled of lemon furniture polish and fried food. Outside, May in Alaska meant the whole state felt warm and green and bursting with life.

Wendy took a deep breath, enjoying the calm before the storm. She had a shift in the ER later.

The controlled chaos of working in trauma care suited her, partly because of her type A personality and partly because being raised in an all-male household meant she'd had to be scrappy to survive. She could take care of herself, could drink and curse with the best of them, could rebuild an engine faster than anyone. And all that independence played nicely into her belief that if she just kept moving, kept busy, kept one step ahead of the game, then her genetics wouldn't catch up with her.

"I'm back," Aiyana said, perching on the edge of her seat like a cello player.

Wendy nodded, shoving her last bite of dessert into her mouth. She wasn't generally the sappy or reflective type, but a tiny part of her wanted to shave off a little of the wonderful closeness Aiyana and Ned shared and hold it inside, so she could turn to it when she felt lonely or desperate. Wendy never stuck around long enough in relationships for things to get that deep.

"How's work?" her sister-in-law asked.

"Same old, same old. Lots of bee stings and weekend warrior accidents this time of year."

She went to say more, but her sister-in-law leaned over again, inhaling deeply. By Wendy's estimation, the contractions were about seven minutes apart, lasting about thirty-eight seconds.

Once the pain passed, Aiyana drank half a glass of water.

"I'm dehydrated," her sister-in-law said, smoothing back her long black ponytail.

And delusional, Wendy thought. These were more than false labor pains. "Sure."

They chatted for a few more minutes and Aiyana snagged one last stray tortilla chip from the nacho tray and shoved it into her mouth. From what Wendy could see, her sister-in-law's belly looked high and tight. Good. As long as it didn't suddenly drop lower, they still had time.

The server delivered their check. "Anything else I can get you, ladies?"

"No, thank you," Aiyana said, then put her head down and took another deep breath.

This contraction was only five minutes from the last one and forty-five seconds long.

Wendy stood and hiked her thumb toward the bathroom. "My turn."

The minute the door closed behind her, she was on the phone to her brother Ned.

"Hello?" his deep baritone answered.

"Hey, bud. It's your little sis."

"Hey." The sounds of a busy garage buzzed in the background. "What's up?"

"I think your wife's in labor. The contractions are coming five to six minutes apart and—well, the last one was forty-five seconds."

Ned's tone shifted from jovial to nervous in one second flat. "That close?"

"Yep. She's claiming they're Braxton Hicks and guzzling water like there's no tomorrow. I'm bringing her in to Anchorage Mercy just in case. I'll call you when we get to the hospital and we'll meet you in the ER."

"Uh, okay," Ned said, his voice strained. "Good thing we got the nursery done last weekend, huh?"

"Yeah." The twins' room was already filled with toys Ned and Aiyana's families had bought over the past few months, with a fondness for oversize Alaskan animals. There was a walrus the size of a small car wedged into the tiny room.

After ending the call, Wendy went back out and paid the check then helped Aiyana stand. Her sister-in-law's face was even redder now, color creeping down her neck and upper chest, the edges of her hairline damp with sweat. Doing her best to keep her tone light, Wendy asked, "Did you have another contraction while I was in the bathroom?"

"I had a twinge."

"A *twinge*?"

"More like a surge."

Twinge and *surge* were used in the natural childbirth community to reference contractions, a way to train their minds to think differently about the pain. Wendy wasn't fooled.

"All right," Aiyana admitted. "Technically, it was a searing, ripping pain, like somebody reached into my belly, twisted it, then wrung it out like a wet shirt."

"And how long did the feeling last?"

"I'm not in labor," Aiyana said, clearly still in denial.

Wendy led her outside and steered her toward the car, parked about half a block away. "Let's walk nice and slowly. It'll help you feel better."

Passersby shot them nervous looks, especially when her sister-in-law cradled her enormous abdomen, teeth gritted as she breathed in and out. Three minutes this time. Wendy counted the seconds, hitting thirty, then forty, then fifty. If they didn't get to Anchorage Mercy soon, the twins would be delivered here on the sidewalk. Wendy shifted into her best take-charge trauma nurse persona. "Aiyana."

"Yes?" her sister-in-law gasped.

"It's time." Despite her bravado, Wendy's voice cracked.

"You're right," her sister-in-law admitted, fear and anticipation sparkling in her deep brown eyes. "Babies are coming."

They stopped talking as another contraction hit, continuing step by painstaking step toward the car. It was going to be a long night.

As far as shifts went, this one was shaping up okay so far, but then, Dr. Thomas Farber still had another nineteen hours to go. He was reserving final judgment until after he got home.

Home. He snorted. His modest two-bedroom apartment in the Rogers Park neighborhood of Anchorage was more like a war zone these days, since his daughter, Samantha, had come to live with him. Not that he didn't love having her there. He did. It was just that he'd expected things between them to be...*different.*

The counselor here at the hospital had told him to be patient, but it was hard when all Tom wanted was to see his daughter smile, laugh, feel comfortable with him and his parents, who lived up in Fairbanks. He wanted her to feel cherished. He wanted to erase that flicker of pain and grief in her green eyes.

A twelve-year-old shouldn't look so world-weary...

His cellphone buzzed in the pocket of his scrubs, distracting him. He pulled it out to see a text from the nanny he'd hired to pick up Sam at the hospital and take her home on the days he worked long shifts. The nanny was running late, but it was fine. Sam could stay in his office and do her homework. He wished he could spend more time with her but keeping a roof over both their heads had to be his top priority right now. Sam understood.

Didn't she?

Tom exhaled slowly and clicked off his phone, guilt squeezing his chest. He sighed and frowned down at his messy handwritten notes in the chart. Honestly, being a single dad was not what he'd expected at all. He wouldn't change it for the world, though. Even if Sam had yelled at him again that morning and told him she hated him.

It was the grief talking. Had to be, right?

The automatic doors at the ambulance entrance to the ER whooshed open and Tom looked up to see a small group of people causing quite a commotion. A heavily pregnant woman, flanked by Dr. Jake Ryder, the head of Emergency Medicine, and a tall man with short, dark hair and a denim work shirt with "Smith's Body Shop and Repair" embroidered on the back.

A nurse walked in behind them. Wendy Smith. She and Tom had said hello in passing a few times after he'd first moved back to Anchorage. In fact, she was the woman who was meeting with Sam for a few weeks in the counselor's absence. He'd meant to introduce himself properly to Wendy, but his workload had kept him too busy.

Following them all was one of the local certified nurse midwives, Carmen Sanchez, and his budding excitement over the prospect of a new case dimmed. He was the OB on call tonight, but unless there were complications severe enough to warrant bringing him in, he probably wouldn't be involved.

They all raced by the nurses' station where he stood. Wendy glanced his way and he couldn't help but notice her long black hair and gorgeous dark eyes. She was curvy and petite, maybe half a foot shorter than his own six-one height.

He had more than enough on his plate at the moment, but couldn't squelch his curiosity about the new case, and found himself tracking the quartet's progress across the busy ER. They loaded onto an elevator, most likely headed for the maternity ward upstairs.

Tom glanced at the dour-faced nurse sitting at the desk before him. "Uh, I think I'll head up to L&D to see if they need help."

"What about the rest of these charts?" the nurse called, her scowl imposing as she pointed at the neat stack of abandoned files he'd left behind.

"I'll get to them later." He backed toward the elevator. "Duty calls."

The doors opened, and he turned to find Wendy blocking his way.

She stared up at him. "Just the man I wanted to see."

He ignored the skip of his pulse and the odd tingle in his bloodstream. It had been so long since anyone had been glad to see him, that had to be it. He swallowed hard and stepped on board the elevator. "What's up?"

"Carmen Sanchez asked for you in Labor and Delivery." Her tone was crisp and clear, like any normal professional nurse-doctor communication, yet it still sent a shiver up Tom's spine.

"Oh. Okay." He did his best to concentrate on the situation and not the woman beside him. Flirting shouldn't even enter into this scenario, no matter how lonely he was. It wasn't the time, and this certainly wasn't the place. "For a consult?"

"Yep." Fear and concern flickered in her dark eyes, mixed with fierce determination. With a curt nod, she pressed the button for L&D and the doors hissed closed, blocking out the chaos of the ER. "My sister-in-law's having twins."

The elevator jolted upward.

"Right. I meant to introduce myself before this, since you're chatting with my daughter, Sam." He extended his hand, feeling awkward. "Tom Farber."

She shook it, her grip strong and sure, her skin soft and warm against his.

Not that he noticed. Nope.

"Of course. Wendy Smith," she said. "Nice to meet you."

CHAPTER TWO

WENDY FELT AS if a fireball had exploded in her body. With one brief touch, this guy had turned her insides into a puddle of goo. An electric charge raced upward from where his palm pressed against hers, warming her, making her throb in parts that had no business throbbing.

She doused those flames fast.

Poor Aiyana was upstairs, about to give birth, and here she was drooling over a hot doc—and Sam's father to boot! Not good. Tom shifted his stance, his arm brushing hers, and fresh sparks fizzed through her body. Trying not to fidget, Wendy studied the metal doors in front of her, doing her best to ignore the hunk beside her and failing miserably.

At last the elevator dinged, and the doors opened.

While Tom talked with one of the delivery nurses, Wendy snuck a closer look at Dr. Tom

Farber. Shaggy blond hair—with highlights of wheat and gold. Bright, intelligent blue eyes that sparkled when he smiled. Tanned, chiseled face, high cheekbones and a shadow of dark stubble on his jaw. Her gaze moved downward to his broad shoulders and muscled arms. He obviously worked out, his faded green scrubs fitting like a glove, not too tight but not baggy either.

Carmen rushed over, her lilting Trinidadian accent low and calm. "Thanks for coming so quickly, Dr. Farber. I need your opinion on a multiple birth."

They all went into Aiyana's room, where she was sitting on a large therapy ball, rocking back and forth. Ned rushed to his wife's side, his emotions written all over his face—panic, compassion, anticipation and a hint of excitement. The guy might be Wendy's own tough older brother, but when it came to his wife's labor, he was a nervous dad-to-be like every other man.

Wendy was there for emotional support, not in a professional capacity. Thankfully, when she'd called Jake earlier he'd told her not to worry about her shift tonight in the ER and to take off all the time she needed to be with her family. Wendy never used her vacation days, so she had plenty saved up.

She and Tom stood at the end of the bed and he reached across her to grab the chart. Golden hair peppered the tanned skin of his muscled forearm, his fingers long and tapered. Surgeon's hands. God, there was something about a man with sexy arms and hands…

Nope. Wendy shook her head, driving away those errant thoughts. She needed to concentrate on providing comfort and coaching to her sister-in-law. That's why she was here. Still, Tom's scent wafted around her—citrus, spice and a hint of soap—smelling better than any man had a right to, darn him.

"Are you okay, *uuman*?" Ned asked Aiyana, rubbing his wife's back.

Tom leaned closer to Wendy, his breath tickling her ear. "What does *uuman* mean?"

She smiled. "It's Iñupiat. It means heart. An endearment."

He nodded, his eyes glittering with interest. "Your family's Native American, then."

"Yes. Half, anyway. Our mom was white."

"I see." He went over Aiyana's chart again, frowning.

Wendy forced her tense shoulders to relax. "Anything to be worried about?"

"No, not that I see. She can continue with Carmen, but I'll keep a close eye anyway." Snapping the file shut, his hand brushed hers and awareness zinged through her once more. Wendy stepped a bit farther away from him, from unwanted temptation.

This was all about birthing the twins, not drooling over Dr. Tall, Blond and Beefcake.

The sooner she got her priorities straight, the better.

Tom put the chart back in the holder, then fiddled with the papers and notes sticking out the sides, ensuring they were all neat and tidy, grateful for something to do with his hands that didn't involve brushing up against Wendy again.

Going over the history and physical, he'd noted that the husband, Wendy's brother, had a family history of Huntington's disease. It was a rare condition and one that had given him pause for a moment. Not out of fear for the patient and her babies—he'd seen that Ned's test results for the mutation had been negative, so there was no concern of him passing it on—but out of concern for Wendy.

He didn't know her that well, neither did he know that much about the disease, only that it was a genetic disorder and that there was no cure. If something that horrible ran in Wendy's family, he couldn't imagine what that must have been like for Wendy, how difficult it would be to live with that hanging over your head.

After the patient returned from the restroom, Ned Smith helped his wife get settled on the bed then tenderly held her hand, calming her. From the chart, Tom had also seen this was their first birth and they were doing well. Aiyana's twins had yet to drop. Between the multiple gestations and the fact that she was a first-time mother, it was going to be a while.

Wendy moved to stand behind her sister-in-law as well, rubbing a tennis ball up and down her lower back. The patient was bent slightly, supported by her husband, her posture stiffening as another contraction hit. They were closer together than Tom had predicted, and he and Carmen exchanged a glance. The midwife tapped her watch and shrugged. He nodded and backed out of the room. If they needed an OB, they'd call him.

Meanwhile, his pulse drummed a steady beat as he studied Wendy more carefully. His respect and admiration for her grew, knowing what she'd dealt with given her family history, while his immediate awareness of her was unsettling for a man who prided himself on being cool, calm and rational. He'd built his life on the known, on facts and science and things that could be measured and tested and applied to provide relief, remedies and comfort.

As Tom rode the elevator back down to the ER, his mind continued to churn—with the case, and with Wendy. Since her father was still alive, according to the chart, he assumed it had been her mother who'd been afflicted with Huntington's. How scary must that have been for young Wendy, being raised with that kind of uncertainty?

The situations were completely different, but the fact Wendy had lost her mother too had

Tom's thoughts returning to his own daughter as he went downstairs to his stack of charts and scribbled note after note in the files, working on autopilot as he searched for new ways he might get Sam to open up and let him in.

His heart ached, though, every time he thought about it—the distance between him and his daughter, the fact his late ex-wife Nikki had blamed him for all her troubles and had kept him and Sam apart. *Regret* wasn't a strong enough word for the thick soup of recriminations that swam inside him when he remembered his short, tumultuous eighteen-month marriage.

After Tom had returned to Alaska, he'd tried to stay in contact with Sam, but Nikki's less-than-stable lifestyle had made communication difficult. He'd even flown back to Boston a few times, hoping to see Sam in person, but Nikki had gone out of her way to keep them apart.

Then Tom had gotten the crushing news from the Massachusetts Department of Family and Children that Nikki had overdosed. He'd returned to the East Coast in a daze, to find Sam in shock. His daughter had looked different than he'd expected, taller, skinnier, tougher.

After the funeral, he'd brought her back to Anchorage, vowing to give her the kind of fairy-tale childhood she'd never had with her mom. New clothes, new school, new whatever she wanted. But with his busy schedule and the emotional trauma she'd suffered, their reunion had been bumpy, to say the least. Between all the social workers and her counselor here at the hospital, he'd expected to see more improvement, but so far it wasn't happening.

It was ironic, really. The fact that he couldn't connect emotionally with his own child, since that was the whole reason he'd gone into obstetrics. That connection that he hadn't been able to have with his own child, that incredible moment when new life emerged.

He wanted to be that bridge of transition forever.

Obstetrics was his calling.

Speaking of his calling, he soon got a page on another case, a VBAC—vaginal birth after C-section.

Glad to stay busy, he headed back upstairs.

CHAPTER THREE

WENDY TRIED TO imagine what the three of them must look like, wandering down the halls of the maternity wing. The walking seemed to help Aiyana. She sipped on a cup of cranberry juice as they strolled at a slow pace. Time and space condensed into *this* hallway, and the *next* hallway, then the one after that. Aiyana had her earbuds in, her attention focused on the music as she shuffled along. She smiled, punching Ned playfully on the shoulder.

"What?" he asked.

"*You* made the playlist."

"I did," he said, grinning from ear to ear.

"Thank you, *paipiirak*." The fact they called each other pet names from their native language was so sweet. Aiyana was his heart while Ned was her baby. Then another contraction hit and Aiyana's face crumpled, her voice shaking. "Here comes another one."

They returned to the room and settled in to wait.

Another hour passed, and Wendy found herself flagging, in desperate need of coffee. She glanced at the clock and found it was nearly four in the morning now. The last time Carmen had checked, Aiyana had been dilated to about six centimeters, but her water still hadn't broken. Without that step, this could take quite a bit longer.

She shook Ned's shoulder as he slept curled in the room's recliner. He mumbled, "Push?"

Wendy snorted. "I'm getting coffee. Want some?"

He shook his head and closed his eyes again, shoving his head against a pillow.

The ride to the basement was eerie this late at night with the place all but deserted. She walked to the cafeteria and grabbed a cup of horrible coffee that would at least buy her a little alert time.

"Hey," a voice said behind her at the register.

She turned to find Tom, his blue eyes twinkling.

"You got some too." He raised the cup in his hands. "Liquid energy."

From what he'd said earlier, he still had a handful of hours left of his shift. He looked as exhausted as she felt. His name tag was askew, hanging from the pocket of his scrubs, and his hair tousled, as if he'd just gotten out of bed. Which made her think of other places he might look so disheveled, say, naked and sleepy between her sheets. And, oh, boy...

Thank goodness he couldn't read minds or they'd both be in trouble.

Then again, Wendy had a feeling being around Tom too much would mean trouble for her no matter what, seeing as how she was drawn to him for no good reason. They barely knew each other and the last thing she wanted was a distraction from what Aiyana was going through.

And Tom Farber was most assuredly distracting.

"Want to sit a minute?" he asked.

She considered turning him down, but the thought of returning to the room upstairs to stare at the same four walls was not appealing. A few more minutes wouldn't hurt anything. "I suppose I can, since Aiyana's sleeping right now."

"Good."

They strolled toward a spot near the back wall of the room.

Tom took the chair across from her at their table for two and Wendy clasped her cup between her hands like a mini-shield between them.

He exhaled slowly and rubbed his eyes. "Maternity must be a nice change from the ER."

"Yep." Wendy watched him closely, noting there was no ring on his finger. No tan line either. Not that she cared. She wasn't interested in his marital status. "What about you? Anything exciting happening in L&D tonight? Besides the impending arrival of the newest members of the Smith clan?"

Tom flashed her a crooked, endearing smile then shook his head. "Nah, not really. I handled a VBAC that got a bit tricky toward the end, but it's all good."

"Cool." Wendy gulped some more coffee, searching for something to say. "Are you from Anchorage originally?"

"I am. Left to go to med school in Boston, but I'm back now. With my daughter, of course."

"Oh, Sam's a great kid." Wendy smiled.

"I think so too. Even if she doesn't think the same about me." He looked at her, his expression a mix of warmth and wariness. "How about you?"

"What? Kids?" Wendy sat back. "Nope. No kids for me."

He chuckled. "No kids now or no kids ever?"

"Ever."

"Okay, then." His smile grew into a grin and the results were dazzling. Warm, friendly, inviting. "I'm sensing some history there. That sounds pretty adamant."

"It is." And that was about as close as he was going to get to her truth. Pulse thumping loud, Wendy stood and hiked her thumb toward the exit, needing to get away from this guy before she did something stupid like tell him all about her Huntington's. She never did that. Ever. Yet there was something about him that made her want to open up. Which was exactly why she had to go. "I, uh, should get back upstairs. Make sure Ned and Aiyana are doing okay."

"Right. Sure." He watched her for a long second, his expression unreadable, then pushed to his feet as well, his movements lithe and graceful. "I'll ride with you. I've got other patients I need to check on."

They walked out into the hallway side by side.

She'd no more than pushed the Up button when the doors opened. He gestured for her to get on first. She did, then fumbled for the right button, feeling awkward and out of sorts. To ease the silence between them, she cracked a joke. "If this was some TV medical drama, we'd be making out between floors."

Wendy cringed, regretting the words the moment they'd left her mouth. God, what was it about this man that made her want to act like a such an idiot? Sure, he was nice and gorgeous and incredibly intriguing. That was no reason to go all gaga over the guy.

Must be the stress of the night. Yep. That's what she was going with anyway.

"Is that an offer?" Tom asked, giving her some serious side-eye.

Okay. The wise thing would've been to ignore that comment and keep her mouth shut until the elevator ride ended. Too bad Wendy wasn't feeling all that smart at the moment, her better judgment apparently having drained away in the wee hours of the morning. Plus, she'd been raised in a houseful of competitive guys and wasn't about to let Dr. McHottiepants get the last word. She arched a brow in his direction, lobbing the ball right back into his court. "Do you want it to be?"

The elevator jolted to a stop, knocking him into her personal space, making heat spark through her nerve endings. His gaze bored into hers, the seconds feeling like minutes.

He took a step back as the doors opened onto the L&D floor again and he held up his hands in defeat, still clutching his coffee. "You win. I'm no good at flirting."

Her reply came out breathier than she'd intended. "Could've fooled me."

She followed him out into the hallway. They stood there dumbly, in the quiet hush of sleeping patients and beeping monitors. Even Aiyana seemed to still be dozing, the door to her room down the corridor closed, no sounds coming from inside.

Tom walked over to the nurses' station and Wendy trailed a step or two behind, her gaze inadvertently dropping down to his rear. Taut and firm, he deserved a trophy for Best Butt Ever.

Ugh. Her rational brain said this would be the perfect time to set him straight in no uncertain terms, to tell him this—whatever *this* was—was nothing.

She was happy with her solitary life, happy without love or commitment or devotion.

Happy not knowing her test results.

Wasn't she?

A loud shriek filled the air, the sound of a mother in the final stages of labor.

Tom's blue eyes widened as he looked back at her over his shoulder.

"Aiyana," they said in unison.

Adrenaline, like a bucket of cold water, splashed over Wendy. She bolted after Tom, running toward her sister-in-law's room, her heart racing as they entered.

"Her water broke," Tom said, staring at the wet floor.

"Carmen just did it," Ned confirmed. He stood

beside his wife now, helping her breathe through the pain. Wendy glanced at the monitors—heart rate, oxygen levels, blood pressure—all normal.

"Looks like we're ready to meet your twins." Carmen proceeded to palpate Aiyana's belly to determine where she was in the process. "The babies have definitely dropped."

A feral growl emerged from Aiyana and with help she stood with her legs wide like a sumo wrestler, her pretty face mottled from her efforts.

"Start pushing," Carmen said.

"She beat you to it," Ned said, holding his wife's upper arm for support.

"I want an epidural!" Aiyana panted after the contraction subsided while Carmen crawled beneath her to place absorbent pads on the linoleum. Given the midwife's stoic expression, she could just as well have been taking a walk in the park, not dealing with a flood.

"We decided to try natural childbirth, *uuman*. Remember?" Ned moved behind Aiyana, his arms ready to slide under hers and catch her if need be. "Besides, Carmen said it's too late."

"I don't—" Aiyana moaned, her head lowered as her belly tightened.

"That's it. That's it," Ned soothed.

"I can't do this!"

"You *are* doing it," Carmen interjected. Aiyana gave the midwife a look of exhausted resignation. "You're going to be a wonderful mother."

Mother.

Out of the blue, the word conjured sudden images of Wendy's own mother reduced to a shell of the woman she'd once been, her once-graceful movements devolving into grotesque twists and jerks, her ever-changing moods and behaviors. That's why Wendy had never gotten her test results, the possibility of dying a horrible, debilitating death and leaving her family behind when they needed her most. That's why she tried never to dwell too much on the future. That's why Wendy coped by picking short-term goals, laser-focusing until they were accomplished. Then she moved on to the next goal and the next. Her goals for the first thirty years of life had been to get through them as far and as fast as she could, with her staunch barriers intact.

Her goals for the next thirty, God willing, were to live like there was no tomorrow.

Because, for her, there might not be.

But with that one simple word all Wendy's yearnings rushed back to the forefront, making her feel as if she'd missed out on a rhythm everyone else could hear.

Suddenly, the world spun, and Wendy grabbed the chair beside her to steady herself. She was a seasoned trauma nurse, had seen more blood and guts than the average soldier, but this was different. Aiyana bore down. Ned supported her. Carmen waited for the emerging baby.

Blackness invaded the edges of Wendy's vision.

Then a pair of strong arms wrapped around her and guided her into the chair.

"It's okay. You're fine," Tom murmured in Wendy's ear, his voice comforting and solid. He settled her, then gently pushed her head between her knees. "Be right back."

He returned with a tiny little cup of water seconds later and pressed it into her hand. "Drink."

"She okay?" Carmen asked from across the room.

This could *not* be happening. Wendy could not fall apart when her family needed her most. Everything was all right. Everything was fine. Everything seemed to be happening around her while she was an orbiting moon, alone. Always alone.

"When was the last time you ate?" Tom placed his hands on her shoulders, kneading her tense muscles, easing her away from the brink.

Food. Wendy thought back to their lunch at the Snaggle Tooth. It seemed like eons ago. She'd had a few bites of dessert, a small portion of nachos, that was all. She shook her head, her mind sluggish, confused. "I... I don't know."

"Hang on." He left the room again.

Aiyana screamed through gritted teeth, the sound visceral.

"That's it, that's it," Carmen said. "You're doing great, Mama."

Next thing Wendy knew Tom shoved a protein bar in her face.

"No." She shook her head, her stomach cramping. Those things tasted like sawdust and paste. Besides, she was feeling a little better now. Not so woozy, head clearer.

"Just take a bite. Trust me. It'll help. You want to be over there with them, right?"

She met his concerned gaze. Embarrassment washed over her again. Yes, she wanted to be over there, wanted to be a part of it all. It was the closest to childbirth she'd likely ever get. "I can't believe this is happening. *I'm a nurse.*"

"It's happened to me too," Tom said, crouching beside her, his hand warm on her knee. "It's different when it's someone close to you."

"Really? You've freaked out when one of your friends gave birth?"

"No, I freaked out when my ex-wife died, and I got custody of my daughter. Now, are we going to chitchat or are you going to eat that and get over there?" Tom asked.

His brisk tone was the wake-up call she needed.

The protein bar was as awful as she'd imagined, but Wendy swallowed it down. Eventually, she felt better, drank the water, then stood, her emotions and the past safely tucked away again. The room stayed in place this time as she held Aiyana's hand, turning back to mouth to Tom, "Thank you."

He smiled and leaned against the doorframe.

Aiyana doubled over again, her face turning a deeper shade of purple.

Carmen gave a thumbs-up. "First baby's head is crowning."

Ned craned over his wife's shoulder, unable to see.

Wendy nodded toward a large mirror on a stand in the corner. "Can we use that?"

"Fine with me," Carmen said. "As long as Mom agrees."

"Aiyana, do you want Ned to see your babies being born?" Wendy asked.

Her sister-in-law nodded, her dark eyes glassy.

Wendy and Tom positioned the mirror so both soon-to-be parents could watch.

The next twenty minutes went by in a blur. A primal scream from Aiyana, the sound of something popping, then a squelching sound as Carmen held baby number one's head and a single shoulder. Aiyana pushed again and soon the sounds of relieved laughter and a newborn baby girl's wail mingled together into a joyful noise. The celebration was short-lived, however, as Aiyana gave a second, determined cry and bore down again. Baby number two entered the world a few minutes later, quivering and covered in muck and crying to his little heart's content.

Carmen handled the squalling little bodies, with the help of a delivery nurse, then placed the infants one by one directly onto Aiyana's chest. Wendy glanced over to see Tom wipe the corners of his eyes before stepping silently from the room.

"They're perfect, *uuman.*" Ned stroked his daughter's head. The baby wrapped four little fingers around his index finger.

Aiyana stared at her twins, eyes wide as she kissed their heads. The boy's mewling cries became a lusty wail as Carmen tucked a warming blanket over each baby.

Wendy couldn't think of a single thing to say,

her heart full to bursting with so many feelings—love, yearning, sadness, relief.

"I did it." Aiyana stroked her son's cheek with her finger and the baby looked up, tiny mouth puckered. Her daughter watched her too, face alert, following her mother's voice.

"You did," Wendy said, smiling through her tears. She leaned in to whisper near her new niece and nephew, "Welcome to the world."

CHAPTER FOUR

TOM WALKED INTO the hospital the next day. Sam was beside him, looking about as happy as dirt. Originally, his plan had been to stop in here quickly to check up on the twins, but his schedule had been interrupted by a call from Sam's school. Seemed she'd gotten caught stealing from the canteen then bolted off school grounds. So he'd trundled himself down to Ryder Academy and offered a nice donation to their booster fund as a way to apologize and appease his guilt.

Bank account lighter, they now strode into Anchorage Mercy ER, Tom dressed in jeans and a polo shirt, and Sam in her school uniform of white shirt and plaid skirt, her attitude belligerent. Tom wasn't feeling too chipper himself at the moment, after his all-night shift.

"What were you thinking?" he asked for the umpteenth time since they'd left the school. "I give you money every morning for lunch, plus an allowance. And leaving school grounds? What were you going to do, hide out in the mountains like Grizzly Adams? Anything could've happened to you. Do you realize that? You scared me half to death."

Sam ignored him, as usual, shuffling forward through the people in the hallway, stopping only to pull her phone from her backpack and jam her earbuds into her ears. Music was her go-to zone these days, using it to block him out. Well, today he wasn't having it.

Tom placed his hand on her shoulder and turned his daughter to face him, tugging on the white cord connecting her earbuds to her phone to yank them from her ears. He took a deep breath to ease the irritation bubbling inside him. Getting upset wouldn't solve anything. Staying calm and rational would win the day, even if she was acting like a stubborn brat. "I'm talking to you, young lady. And this time you're going to listen."

Several people jostled around them, and Tom realized they were blocking the elevators. Muttering his apologies, he steered Sam over to the side of the corridor, where she stood with her arms crossed, refusing to meet his gaze.

His heart ached for her, but this needed to be said, one way or another. "Your behavior today is unacceptable. I know how much you miss your mother, but I'm doing my best here, Sam. I'm sorry you were ripped away from your life in Boston and forced to come here to the Great White North. I'm sorry I work such long hours to support us both. I'm sorry."

He raked a hand through his hair, not missing the fact people were glancing their way and whispering. His perfectionist tendencies reared their ugly head, making him feel like even more of an idiot. This wasn't what he wanted, wasn't the kind of relationship he yearned for with his daughter. "Please, help me out here. We're a family now. I'm doing the best I can, okay?"

Sam had lost a lot, yes, but he'd tried so hard to make sure she was well taken care of, tried to make sure she was happy, tried to ensure she was clothed and comfortable and fed. On the days he was home, they had dinner together. Like the other night, he'd brought home pizza. But the minute he'd walked in the door, Sam had declared she wanted Thai food instead. Eager to please, Tom had traipsed back down to buy pad Thai, but that hadn't satisfied her either. By the time he'd gotten home, his daughter had changed her mind again and wanted burgers.

Frustrated, he ran a hand through his hair. "Maybe I should start coming to your counseling appointments with you. Or those chats you have in the cafeteria. Maybe that would help us communicate better."

"No. I don't want you at my counseling appointments. And I don't want you in the cafeteria either," Sam said, her tone seething. "I sat in the principal's office for two hours."

"Because I was finishing my shift and I had to arrange for another doctor to take over while I went in to get you. I can't just leave my patients hanging."

"But it's fine to do to me, huh?" She glared at him. "You only care about you."

He gave an aggrieved sigh. "Why, Sam? Tell me why you thought it was okay to steal."

The next thing he knew, Sam pushed away from the wall and broke into a run down the hallway, the rubber soles of her shoes squeaking loudly on the linoleum.

"Dammit." Tom took off after her. "Samantha Jane Farber. Wait!"

She didn't.

Sam rounded the corner and Tom sped up, arriving in time to see the door to the unisex bathroom slam shut. The lock clicked into place with a loud, echoing *snick*.

With as much dignity as he could muster, Tom strode over to the door and knocked. "Sam, please come out. This isn't the way to handle an argument."

"Stop telling me what to do and how to feel. Mom was right. You aren't God. You don't control everything," Sam yelled through the door. "No wonder she left you."

Stunned and hurt, Tom leaned back against the opposite wall. This was not going well. They needed to talk about things, needed to apologize and move forward, which Tom fully intended to do once his daughter emerged. If she came out. But the seconds turned into minutes and his hopes dwindled. He wasn't trying to be God. If anything, he'd done his best not to allow his controlling tendencies free rein. But stealing was a serious offense. He only wanted to talk to Sam, to make her understand where he was coming from, to keep her safe.

He paced. He stretched his tense arms and rolled his tense shoulders. Tension knotted inside him, coiling tighter and tighter as the time ticked by. Never had he felt so totally, overwhelmingly, embarrassingly inept.

"Sam, please," he tried again, pleading to her through the door.

Nothing.

Tom checked the knob. Still locked. "Please come out. I'm sorry."

No response.

Out of alternatives, he started back toward the nurses' station, checking over his shoulder every so many steps to see if Sam emerged. No luck. Tom stopped at the same desk where he'd been documenting in his charts the day before and spoke to the nurse on duty. "Can you call Maintenance, please? I need the door to the bathroom in the rear corridor opened."

The nurse gave him a flat look then reluctantly picked up her phone to dial. "Sure. 'Cos

I don't have anything better to do than play operator for you, Doc."

Tom thanked her. He could've done without the added snark today, but at this point he'd take whatever help he could get. A few minutes later the nurse informed him Maintenance would be on their way shortly. He headed back toward the bathroom. Usually they were here within fifteen minutes, tops. This wasn't the first time he'd had to call them for this situation, unfortunately. Hopefully Sam hadn't bolted again already.

Man, the thought of her running away and roaming the streets of Anchorage made his chest squeeze with fear. Not that Anchorage wasn't a safe city, but a twelve-year-old girl alone in the world was a recipe for disaster.

Then Tom rounded the corner and found Wendy standing in the hallway, talking to Sam. She was dressed casually today too, in a pink skirt and a black short-sleeved sweater. As he drew closer, he picked up snippets of their conversation.

"The fox was starving," Sam said. "They were throwing out that old food anyway. Besides, if my dad's mad enough at me, then maybe he won't make me go to Fairbanks. I'll probably just embarrass him in front of his parents anyway. I told you yesterday at lunch I didn't want to go and now hopefully I won't have to."

"Wait a minute," Tom said, approaching them. "Seriously? That's what this was all about? To get out of a trip to see your grandparents?"

"It wasn't stealing if they were going to throw it out anyway." Sam swiveled to face him, arms still crossed, her expression defiant. "And I told you I don't want to go to Fairbanks. Leave Wendy alone."

"The plans are made, and my parents are excited to see you. The fresh air will do you good. You're going. End of story." Over the Memorial Day long weekend. Because they both needed a break and Tom needed to figure out a new approach to handling his daughter.

"You just want to get rid of me." Sam took a step closer to Wendy as though she needed protection from him. "He doesn't want me. He never wanted me. My mom told me so. Now she's dead and I'm all alone."

Tom's heart sank. How could she think that? He wanted her more than anything else on this earth. He'd worked so hard to prove that to her. He reached for her, wanting to hold her, comfort her. "Sam, please."

"No!" His daughter flinched away, her breathing rough as she continued to plead her case to Wendy. "He says I have to stay with them, no matter what, for four whole days. He says I can't come home early, under any circumstances."

"Because I have to work."

"That's all you do is work!" Sam yelled. "He hates me."

Wendy snorted and shook her head. "Sorry, but the overdramatics are killing it, kid."

Shocked, Sam stared up at her with wide eyes. "I'm totally serious. He all but said so right before you got here."

"I never—"

"Wow." Wendy gave Tom a quick glance, her droll tone adding a much-needed dose of coolness to the heated situation. "And all this time I've been telling Sam you couldn't possibly be as big a jerk as she said." She snorted. "Guess

I stand corrected, even if you did help deliver my niece and nephew."

Tom stood there, unable to stop staring at Wendy. At first, he'd thought he must have imagined how pretty she was, given his level of exhaustion last night. But now she was oozing natural beauty and intelligence and charm...

He lost track of the conversation for a moment.

"If he makes me go," Sam said, snapping him right back into reality, "I'll run away."

"No, you won't," Wendy said, her tone firm with authority, in full nurse mode now.

"Why not?" Sam said. "You told me you thought about doing it, after your mom died."

Wendy gave his daughter a flat stare, not budging an inch. "I also told you I didn't do it, because running away is a stupid move. Your problems have a way of finding you eventually."

Sam grumbled under her breath and turned away.

"Hey, look at me," Wendy said. "Sam?"

Slowly, his daughter turned back around, and beneath all his daughter's tough preteen angst

Tom saw a vulnerable, sad little girl. Talk about a sucker punch in the feelings.

"Listen, you're not alone. You've got me." Wendy took a business card out of the pocket of her skirt and scribbled something on the back with a pen before passing it to Sam. "My work number is on the front and my cell number is on the back. Promise you'll call me anytime, for any reason, okay?"

Wendy's phone buzzed, and she pulled it out. "Saved by the text message. Ned's looking for me upstairs." She walked away, then turned back, her dark gaze flickering over Tom before landing on his daughter once more. "See you around, Sam."

Ugh. Wendy let her head fall back against the wall of the elevator as she rode upstairs.

Great. Now she felt even more off-kilter, both from seeing Sam so upset and the electric jolt of her persistent attraction to Tom, still there, stronger than ever.

She'd tried to convince herself that her awareness of him had been due to the adrenaline rush of Aiyana's delivery. That she'd only imagined his gorgeousness and her strong, physical reactions to him, but nope. Her rational brain was still reeling from seeing him again and a tingling trail of sizzling expectation still sparkled like fireworks inside her core.

Which was so bad, considering her sessions with Sam.

Sam...

For the past few weeks, during her shifts in the ER, Wendy had taken a late lunch, heading down to the cafeteria around three. The place was less crowded, quieter then, and she met with the girl. Afterward, she wrote copious notes to report on Sam's progress and anything of a troubling nature. At first, the worst thing Wendy had uncovered was her growing infatuation with a cute boy in her class.

But lately, as the bond of trust between them had grown stronger, Sam had started talking about her mother back in Boston and what had happened, slowly letting go of the hurt and pain. There was definitely a lot of baggage the girl and her dad needed to unpack, if their interaction today in the hallway was any indication, but they were making progress.

The elevator dinged, and Wendy stepped off into the busy maternity ward lobby, spotting Ned walking toward her from the direction of the gift shop with yet more stuffed animals under his arms—this time a seal pup and a penguin.

"More animals for the twins?" she said. "They've got enough already to start a zoo."

"Hey, I'm a proud papa. What can I say?" Ned shrugged, looking both exhausted and energized. She was proud of her brother for keeping it together so well, until she glanced down and realized he was wearing two different shoes. Last night had been tough on all of them.

"Those things won't fit in a bassinet." She chuckled. "In fact, you'll be lucky if they fit through the door, bro."

They walked toward Aiyana's room, then Ned stopped off to talk to the nurses at the desk. Wendy went on ahead into her sister-in-law's room, finding the new mother sitting in bed with a twin in each arm, both babies freshly diapered and wrapped tightly in their little burrito blankets.

"Hey." Wendy waved. "How's it going this morning?"

Aiyana smiled serenely, like she'd always had two snoozing infants in her arms. Wendy tamped down the pinch of grief in her heart. Her decision not to have children was the right one for her. No sense doubting it now. Besides, she preferred solid certainty to openness and vulnerability any day of the week.

Don't I?

The sleeping babies startled, and Aiyana quickly nestled them closer to her chest, beckoning Wendy over to the chair beside the bed. The babies fell back asleep, their little breaths even and deep.

Aiyana looked almost as tired as Ned, her pretty face puffy and swollen, tiny blood vessels around her eyes and cheeks bright red. Her expression was joyful, though, and it was contagious, seeping into Wendy, replacing the tension inside her from seeing Tom again.

"They're so beautiful," her sister-in-law whispered. "I never imagined it would feel like this, so real and right and true."

"They are," Wendy said, admiring her little niece and nephew, feeling a weird knot of yearning inside her. Babies needed constant attention. Babies needed protection and nurturing. All the things her father and brothers had done their best to provide for her. All the things she'd missed so desperately from her own mother. Since Wendy couldn't guarantee she could provide that to her own children, it was best for her not to have them at all.

No matter how much being here today might make her want kids of her own.

You could get the test results. If they're negative, you could have babies.

Yeah, no. Better to keep her barriers in place and forget her pipe dreams.

Allowing someone close, allowing a man into her heart, risked too much.

What if she got sick? What if the impossible happened and she got pregnant?

What if she died, abandoning her baby and her husband?

What if...?

Yet as Wendy sat there, watching Aiyana and the twins, she felt a burning pang of melancholy. The most vivid memories she had of her mother were those from when she'd been too tired and sick to move. How could she put her loved ones through that? She couldn't.

Her life was good the way it was.

It was all good.

It was what she'd wanted. No commitments, no strings. No heartache.

"It's scary too," Aiyana said, as if reading Wendy's mind. "This is only the first day and there isn't a manual." She glanced over at the nightstand where there was a teetering pile of books left by well-meaning staffers and friends. "No. That's not true. There are actually thousands of manuals. What I mean is, the books tell the basics, but there's no minute-by-minute breakdown. You have to figure it out as you go along, but it's so worth it."

Pulse stuttering, Wendy swallowed hard. This wasn't the conversation she wanted to have today, especially now with so many memories and emotions and everything feeling too overwhelming.

"How are you feeling today?" Wendy changed the subject, her gaze on the twins, with their swollen eyelids and little dots of baby acne all over their faces. Aiyana pulled off her daughter's pink cotton cap and smoothed the shock of black hair on her head then did the same for her son, revealing a tiny scalp full of dark curls, just like Ned's. The sweetness of the moment nearly broke Wendy's heart.

"Want to hold one?" Aiyana leaned forward, wincing as she shifted.

Carefully, Wendy took the boy, supporting his tiny body. He felt so light, just over five pounds. Then he snuggled and sighed against her arm and warmth surged inside her. She kissed his little head, inhaling his good baby smell.

"Names?" Wendy asked again.

"Well, we're thinking about—" Aiyana turned toward the door. "Is that you, *paipi-irak*?"

As if on cue, the giant stuffed head of a penguin peeked into the room. Ned followed.

Wendy grinned at the tiny baby in her arms. "That crazy guy's your dad. He has the worst taste in toys. You'll have to deal with it. Sorry, little bud. The deck is stacked against you.

Good thing you have your aunt Wendy to keep you normal."

The adults in the room snorted in unison.

Then there was a quiet knock on the door and there stood Tom Farber, sans Sam. Wendy leaned slightly to see if his daughter would follow but she didn't. Had she run away again? No. Tom would've looked a lot more panicked if that were the case. Instead, he just looked decidedly too handsome for his own good. The way that navy blue polo shirt and those faded jeans fit his body should be illegal. Wendy looked away before things got weird.

Her brother, of course, managed to take it right over the cliff into mortifying territory. "Yeah, right, sis. You wouldn't know normal if it bit you in the butt. Kids, your aunt here dangled off a cliff at O'Malley's Peak just to win a dare. Sorry, but that's not normal, Wen. It's—"

"Shh." Aiyana narrowed her gaze on their new guest. "Hi, there... I'm sorry. I forgot your name."

"Tom. Dr. Tom Farber. I was the OB on call last night. Hope I'm not interrupting." He shook

Aiyana's hand then looked at Wendy. "You dangle off cliffs a lot?"

"No." Wendy shot visual daggers at her brother. "Well, I mean, yes. Sometimes. I volunteer with the local Anchorage rescue team once a month, but it's not nearly as interesting as it sounds. And the bet was Jake Ryder's idea, if you really want to know."

Tom managed to keep his expression impassive, but she didn't miss the amused glint in his blue eyes. "Right."

"Where's Sam?" Wendy asked, ignoring the possibilities shimmering in the air between them.

"The nanny took her back to my apartment since she's suspended from school for the rest of the day." At Aiyana and Ned's curious looks, he clarified, "Samantha's my twelve-year-old daughter. It's a long story." A slight blush stained his tanned, chiseled cheekbones. He pointed toward the remaining twin in Aiyana's arms. "May I?"

Her sister-in-law looked as flustered as Wendy felt under Tom's dazzling grin. "Sure."

Tom carefully lifted the snoozing baby girl

into his arms, looking downright dapper today, all clean shaven and hair styled. For a guy whose interactions with his own daughter had been rocky at best, he seemed completely comfortable with the twins. She felt sorry for him, and for Sam, that they hadn't yet found that easy sort of relationship. She didn't imagine the current tense scenario was good for either of them.

Sam's impassioned words popped back into her head.

She's dead and I'm all alone...

Her gaze drifted down to the sleeping infant in her arms. The tiny, helpless baby whose entire existence currently rested on Wendy. Emotional paralysis set in with alarming swiftness, making her muscles freeze. That sickening dizziness from the night before raced back. Her hands shook, her mouth dried.

"Wendy?" Tom asked, watching her closely. His voice was quiet and soothing, cutting through her gathering panic, the same as it had the previous evening. "You look a bit pale. Everything okay?"

Thankfully, her years of nurse's training and

instinct kicked in. Wendy handed her nephew back to Aiyana, then stood on shaky legs. "Uh, excuse me a sec. Be right back."

She made her way out of the room, deeply humiliated and embarrassed. Once she was alone in the hallway, the violent tremors started. She tried to walk them off, searching for a water fountain. Finally locating it, she moved robotically, her body stiff with purpose and old grief.

As she drank greedily, her thoughts swirled. Resignation stabbed through her, wounds buried so deep she had no desire to dig everything up again. Yet here she was, her old childhood tragedies and new fears for the future smacking up against what was supposed to be a joyful day for her family.

"Wendy?" Tom's deep voice behind her felt like an embrace, though he stood far enough away to give her some privacy. She felt a wild urge to throw her arms around him, have him comfort the confusion out of her. Once again, she felt the unaccountable urge to *talk* to him, to confide in him what was going on inside her. Tell him about the dreaded disease that ran in her family, lurking like a phantom over every facet of her personal life. Then again, he'd seen Aiyana's chart the night before, so he probably knew already. Maybe that's why he'd been frowning...

She swallowed hard against the lump constricting her throat. She barely knew the guy, and the fact he was a good doctor and a struggling father didn't mean she could trust him with her deepest fears and secrets. She took an extra gulp of water to help force down her feelings.

"Wendy?" Tom said again, and she closed her eyes.

Damn. He wasn't going to let this go.

Finally, she pivoted to face him. "I'm fine... I don't even know what that was."

Tears stung her eyes before she blinked them away.

"I do." His gaze held empathy and understanding. "If you want to talk about the Huntington's, I'm here."

He knew. She snorted to cover the raging tempest inside her about that fact, feeling too vulnerable for her comfort. "I'm fine."

"If you say so." He stepped closer, bridging

the gap between them to brush away a lock of hair that had fallen in front of her face. Her breath hitched against her will. "I can't imagine what it must be like, what you've been through. You try to hide your soft underbelly, but I see it. Maybe that's why you got through to Sam when I couldn't. Maybe that's why you almost fainted last night too, why you locked up just now holding the baby. Stress. Fear."

"I did not lock up when I was holding that baby," Wendy hissed, scowling. "That's ridiculous. I'm a nurse. I've held hundreds of babies."

"Uh-huh." He narrowed his gaze on her, looking entirely unconvinced. His fingertips grazed her jaw and her earlier tension gave way to a whole new kind of tightness. The same connection from last night sizzled between them again. Tom moved close enough for her to see the shadow of stubble on his jaw, close enough for his minty breath to fan her face, close enough for her to feel the heat of him through her clothes. She stared up at him, wide-eyed, like a rabbit in a trap. He bent toward her. At first, she thought he was going to kiss her, and her heart nearly beat right out of her chest. Then he stopped and lowered his voice, making her shiver. "I think we should talk."

"What?" she squeaked out, her lips still tingling in anticipation of his kiss.

He leaned back slightly to meet her eyes, his gaze glittering with a mix of interest and wariness. "About Sam, of course."

Of course.

"Wendy?" Aiyana's voice jarred her out of his spell. "Are you okay?"

"She's fine," Tom answered, stepping back to reveal her sister-in-law standing in the doorway to her room at the end of the hall. He turned back to Wendy. "Ready?"

"I can't talk to you about Sam's case," she said, regretting the sharp words as soon as they emerged. She didn't want to lash out at Tom, but he made her feel so damned weak and defenseless. Bad enough she lost all control over her reactions to him whenever he was around. "You'll need to ask your daughter. Or the counselor."

She headed back toward her sister-in-law's room without waiting to see if he followed.

He did, his presence behind her sending more waves of sizzling awareness through her, darn him.

Thankfully, Aiyana didn't seem to pick up on the tension now brewing between them as she gushed over Tom. "Wow. You're such a good doctor, taking care of Wendy like that when it's not even your job."

Wendy managed to suppress her eye roll, barely.

Fine. Yes. The guy really was perfect. Tall, gorgeous, smart, funny, caring. Didn't mean she should melt into a puddle of goo each time he walked into the room. Especially since he knew about her disease. Or potential disease. Or whatever.

She couldn't think straight around him. Which only made her feel more annoyed.

A loud, lusty cry came from the bassinets and Aiyana reached over to pick up one of the twins. Ned yawned from where he sat beside the bed, covering his mouth and apologizing in muffled tones. "I'm going to get some real sleep as soon as the babies settle down," he said. "Aiyana can rest too, while the staff here takes care of the twins—" He stopped short as his wife began singing a lullaby. The baby quieted and focused cloudy, bluish-brown eyes on her.

Yearning intensified inside Wendy, making it hard to breathe, making her want to crawl out of her own skin. She edged toward the door, bumping into Tom. "I'm going to get some air. See you later."

Looking confused, Aiyana frowned. "But you just came back in."

Tom took her arm and smiled. "We're going for a walk together. Right?"

Part of Wendy wanted to go with him, very much. But the other part of her wanted to run far and fast, knowing he wasn't the man for her and getting any more involved in his life and the life of his daughter would only cause trouble, mainly for her and her heart.

She didn't do long-term relationships and Tom had forever written all over him.

But he knows about the Huntington's and he hasn't fled. He's still here.

In the end, it was that curiosity that won out over her self-preservation. Besides, getting out of the hospital would probably go a long way toward helping her figure out how the hell she could get back to some semblance of stable. Wendy nodded. "Right."

CHAPTER FIVE

AS THEY RODE the elevator down to the main entrance, Wendy's mind raced through a million different scenarios, most of them involving either being pinned to the wall of the elevator by Tom, darn him, or her telling him to butt out of her life. She wasn't sure which would be better at this point.

"Want to grab a coffee while we're out?" he asked. "Talk about things?"

"The nearest coffee shop is five blocks away." She swallowed hard as the elevator dinged and they walked out into the sunlit atrium.

"I know. I'm good with it if you are. Give us more time to get to know one another."

That set her back a notch. She'd expected a simple, short stroll around the hospital campus, perhaps a few questions about her family history, but now this felt almost more like a... *date*. Still, it was too late to back out now and she didn't want him to know how flustered he made her feel.

They strolled along through the beautiful May day, him accommodating her shorter strides. Even with her emotions all topsy-turvy, she couldn't help admiring the way his shirt outlined his buff torso or how those jeans cupped his taut thighs perfectly.

She wanted to come off as confident, because she felt anything but with this guy. She wasn't beautiful, not in the conventional sense. She was a bit too curvy, a tad too feisty for most men to handle. And, yeah, maybe she'd been told she resembled Ashley Callingbull. Sure. Maybe, if model Ashley was four inches shorter, a few pounds heavier and a lot less stunning.

Then again, those same men who'd lavished her with compliments were the same ones who'd hightailed it out of there once they'd learned how many hours Wendy worked or the fact she knew more about engines, spark plugs and fuel lines than they did.

Maybe Tom's different...

Except she wasn't going there, because of her past and because of his present with Sam.

Dogwoods flowered around them as they walked through a residential neighborhood. He tipped his handsome face skyward, soaking up the sun. A light breeze ruffled her hair and her tense muscles relaxed, despite all her inner turmoil.

They traveled in pleasant silence for a few blocks before he turned to her with a sad smile. "I shouldn't say this, but I'm actually glad you're the one meeting with Sam. She needs a friend right now and it looks like you've got the job. I've tried everything I know to get her to let me in, but so far she won't. You two have a lot in common, though, huh?" His cheeks flushed. "Sorry. I shouldn't have asked that. Out of bounds."

He looked so darned adorable that she caved a bit. She couldn't discuss specifics with him. That was just asking for trouble. But she could throw him a bone, in general. "Girls her age are a mystery wrapped in an enigma," Wendy said, skirting his question. At his flat stare, she laughed. "It's true. Take it from someone who was once a twelve-year-old girl herself. Seriously, though, have you considered you might be trying too hard? Give her some space. Don't try to force her to accept you and all this new stuff. Just be there for her. Talk to her like you would any other person in her situation. She'll come around eventually."

"You sound so confident about that, but I'm not sure." He seemed to consider her response a moment, frowning down at the sidewalk. "It doesn't feel like it will be fine. Most of the time it feels like I'm walking through land mines waiting for the next one to explode. This isn't how I usually like things to be in my life. I tend to be a bit of a perfectionist."

"I've noticed." At his sideways glance she gave him a half smile. "From the way you straighten things all the time. And that quality's great for when you're being Dr. Tom Farber, obstetrician extraordinaire. Not so much when you're trying to be Dad Tom or a good friend to your daughter." At his crestfallen look, Wendy took pity on him and laid her hand on his arm. "Sam doesn't expect or want you to be perfect. All she wants is for you to be there for her. To know you'll support her when she needs you, physically and emotionally."

"Easier said than done. There's only so many hours in the day and I work long shifts. I want so badly to do what's best for Sam, but I also have to think about our future. She's my responsibility now."

"Have you shared your concerns with her?" Wendy asked as they crossed another street. "If not, maybe you should. Might help her understand why you're doing what you do and let her know you care. She's twelve, Tom, not two. She'll understand. Probably more than you think."

Wendy exhaled slowly, filtering through her words, deciding what to say and what not to. Tom really was so easy to talk to, though, and he seemed so eager to make his daughter happy. It wasn't the ideal situation, but maybe if she told him a bit more about herself, he'd ease up on the subject of what she and Sam discussed. "Like you said, we have a lot of things in common. I lost my mother too. When I was ten."

She took off toward the coffee shop again. Mainly to avoid what would probably be a look of pity on his face. That was the usual reaction she got when people found out about her past. And the last thing she wanted from him was pity.

Tom followed behind her, a few paces back, and Wendy hazarded a glance at his face. No pity, thank goodness. Just golden, gorgeous male. That unwanted zing of awareness seared hotter inside her, urging her to say something, anything, to keep from tackling him to the grass and kissing him silly. "How long were you married to Sam's mom?"

"Eighteen months. We met while I was in medical school in Boston. She was a local artist. Fantastically talented painter, but sometimes genius comes with a price." At Wendy's pointed look, he continued. "I didn't know she was an addict until after we took our vows. She hid it well, but things went downhill from the honeymoon onward. I tried to get her to go to rehab, and she didn't use at all when she was pregnant with Sam. Afterward, though, it was a different story." He exhaled slowly and stared across the street while they waited for the light.

"Despite what my daughter might have told

you, I wanted to be a part of Sam's life. In fact, I spent years trying to see her after our divorce, but Nikki wouldn't let me. She'd conned the judge into giving her full custody, so legally, I was dependent on her cooperation. By the time I got the job offer from Anchorage Mercy, Nikki was doing well for herself, selling some of her artwork, off the drugs again. But things between us, communication-wise, had deteriorated to the point that she was threatening to get a restraining order against me if I tried to see Sam. So I moved back here, reluctantly. Putting a continent between me and Sam wasn't ideal, but I never imagined the price I'd pay." The light turned green and he sighed, his smile strained.

"I've tried to do my best with my daughter in this difficult situation, but it seems all I've done is screw up worse, make the same mistakes. With the emotional canyon between us now, it feels like things were doomed from the start."

They entered the downtown area and weaved through the crowds of tourists milling about the streets of Anchorage, admiring the quaint shops and scenery. Tom stopped to peer into the window of an art gallery. "I'm sorry about your mother."

His gentle words were like a stab in the gut. It had been twenty years since her mother had passed away, yet the quiet comfort in Tom's tone made Wendy want to bury her face in his broad, muscled chest. Which wasn't going to happen, no matter how appealing his smile was, or how good he smelled, or the fact that he looked like some Norse god come to life.

She kept her distance for a reason and she intended for things to stay that way.

Definitely. Maybe.

Ugh.

"Thanks," she managed to say while staring at a huge watercolor portrait of a grizzly bear devouring a salmon in a stream. "It was a hard time. She went downhill pretty quickly toward the end. It was difficult to watch, especially as a kid."

Sam had gone through some tough times with her mother too, nights when she'd come home late and strung out. Or the nights she'd not come home at all. That was one of the new things Sam had opened up to Wendy about recently, amid all their usual talk about her new school, her homework, the cute boy she liked.

Sam had also mentioned how much she missed Boston and her mother and how she felt like her dad didn't understand anything. Wendy wouldn't mention any of that to Tom, though. It had to come from Sam or the counselor. Besides, it would also only hurt him more, which would make Wendy want to hug and comfort him and that was far too unsettling to contemplate.

Still, the thought of poor Sam all alone in that Boston apartment, crying herself to sleep, hit far too close to home for Wendy. Not that she'd ever been abandoned, but she'd soaked many a pillow with tears over her mother's death, terrified the same fate would befall her someday. She held her breath, waiting for more inevitable questions from Tom about her mother's disease, questions she'd have to answer now since she'd basically brought it up in the first place.

"Have you had the testing done?" he said, his voice barely a whisper above the din of the busy street behind them. "If you don't mind me asking."

Normally, she did mind. Very much. Being asked that felt like an invasion of privacy.

But with Tom her chest didn't tighten, her heart didn't ache.

Strange, but she wasn't ready to consider exactly why at the moment.

Wendy blinked away the unwanted sting of tears. "I did. When I was eighteen."

Tom looked away, but not before she saw the flicker of concern in his eyes. Her heart sank. Any attraction he felt for her now would certainly be gone. Best to swim far away from that tainted gene pool.

They walked on. Tom thankfully changed the topic. "You're from Anchorage too?"

"Born and raised," she said, squinting into the sunlight. "My family owns a garage on the outskirts of town."

"That's where your brother's shirt came from last night. I meant to ask him today." He paused, his expression curious. "And your family's part Iñupiat?"

"Yep." She chuckled, glad to have an easier topic to discuss. "Or as Jake likes to say—I'm half Iñupiat and all attitude. My mother was from Michigan. She came here on an Alaskan cruise and met my dad and never went back." She ignored the familiar stab of sadness in her chest as their destination loomed ahead. "There's the coffee shop."

He watched her closely. "What's your favorite drink?"

"Coffee-wise, you mean?"

"Yeah. Wait." Tom held up a hand, flashing his gorgeous grin. "Let me guess."

She planted her hands on her hips. "Go for it."

"I'd say you're a...latte gal."

Damn. He was correct, but she wasn't sure if she wanted him to know it. Having him off-balance again felt way more comfortable.

"C'mon, I'm right, aren't I?"

She looked up at him. "Fine. Yes. Lattes. Occasionally, I'll have a triple if I need the extra caffeine, but..."

"Espresso doesn't have as much caffeine as you'd think," they said in unison.

"You *know* that?"

"*You* know that?" he countered, giving her a crooked smile. And darn if she didn't feel it all the way to her toes. Then there was the fact

Tom seemed to be taking all this new information about her in his stride, at least for now. It was weird, and oddly refreshing.

"Now guess my drink," he said as they made their way into the coffee shop.

"Well, I know you like it with milk, from last night."

The barista looked at them expectantly. This was an independent coffeehouse, built into what had once been a barber shop. The long, narrow space was shabby chic, with painted chalkboard walls and a handwritten menu. The big star was the espresso machine, all shiny copper and steel gears, like something from a steampunk fantasy.

Tom remained focused on Wendy, waiting for her answer. She looked him up and down, thinking of what she'd heard about him from Sam and what he'd told her in their brief time together.

"Macchiato."

His brows knit. "What?"

"You're a macchiato guy."

He crossed his arms, his expression skeptical. "How'd you know? Did Sam tell you?"

"No. She didn't have to." Wendy gave a short laugh, leaning against the counter. "You're strong, steadfast, maybe even a little stubborn. You prefer facts and details. You pride yourself on your control and you're responsible to a fault. You work hard, maybe too hard."

"Guilty as charged." Tom turned to the barista. "A latte and a macchiato, please."

They nabbed one of the few tables left, most of the spots taken by people using the place as a pseudo-office. Wendy sat down, fumbling to know what to do with her hands, what to feel about all the odd emotions racing through her in Tom's presence—attraction, irritation, lust, wariness. He was just too darned likable, that was the problem. And for Wendy, who avoided commitment like a bad MRSA infection, liking Tom could easily lead to deeper feelings and *that* scared the hell out of her.

This was exactly why she stuck to flings.

No mess, no worry, no chance of emotions or hearts involved.

No chance of passing on a deadly disease or leaving a grief-stricken spouse behind.

Then Tom shifted in his seat and leaned forward across the small table to take her hand unexpectedly. His skin felt soft and warm against hers, his grip strong, firm, the kind a girl could rely on. It was then Wendy realized she was in far more danger with him than she'd ever been with any of the previous guys she'd been around.

"I want to thank you for being Sam's friend," Tom said, surprising her. "Thanks for being there for her. I know I shouldn't be saying any of this, but it means the world to me. Truly. Thank you." He held her gaze a moment before releasing her hand and sitting back in his seat. "And I know this will probably break all the rules, but I'd like your help too. I want you to teach me how to be a better father to my daughter. If you'll agree."

Oh, boy. Her pulse quickened at his words.

Which was both so very bad and yet so, so good.

It had been forever since she'd had a male friend, other than Jake. Forever since she'd let a man into her life, period, beyond a one-night stand, beyond just physical intimacy. Forever since she'd felt such a bright buzz of attraction and wasn't scared out of her wits, even knowing how it would end.

Common sense said she should say no, should stay the course, keep to her narrow, lonely path. But, crazy as it sounded, Tom seemed to get her. And the counselor was due back from vacation next week, so that took care of any conflict of interest issues. Wendy didn't know how or why she felt so drawn to Tom, but she was intrigued enough to stick around and find out. "Okay."

Hard to believe one simple word meant so much to him.

Okay.

The knots between his shoulder blades eased slightly, knowing she'd agreed to help him.

Honestly, if Tom could've hit pause on Wendy's macchiato explanation of him, he would have. Frankly, he'd been shocked by her accurate description, like she'd cracked his chest open to reveal his beating heart. Macchiatos were, in fact, his favorite coffee. He wanted to ask her more about herself too, but just then the barista called, "Tom!"

He jumped up and motioned for Wendy to wait while he got their order. Returning, he carefully set everything down. They each sipped their drinks and he watched her over the rim of his cup. She seemed nervous and he didn't want to push, like he always did, but he couldn't avoid the huge white elephant in the room either. After all, he'd ignored the issues right in front of his face with Nikki and he didn't want to do that again. He'd learned the hard way that the only way around problems was through them. "So, you had the testing done, what, twelve years ago?"

Wendy blinked fast, staring down into her coffee. She looked so vulnerable and sad he wanted to pull her into his arms and tell her everything would be okay, even if it wouldn't.

She nodded but didn't say anything more, just fiddled with her drink.

His gut went into a nosedive, thinking the worst. "Oh, I'm so sorry. I didn't realize. I never would've asked if I'd known you were—"

That got her attention at last. She gave him a pointed stare. "I'm not dying, for goodness' sake." Wendy gave a quick glance around, realizing she'd probably said that way louder than necessary. "At least I don't think I am. I don't know. I haven't gotten my results."

Now it was Tom's turn to blink. He forced his gaping mouth to close and took that in for a minute. "You had the testing done but didn't want to know the results, after all these years?"

She stared down at the table, a slight blush dotting her high cheekbones.

"Wow." He couldn't imagine living with that kind of uncertainty. Perhaps that explained why Wendy kept her distance from others. Probably also explained why such a smart, beautiful woman was still unattached.

Some men might have balked, but Tom just marveled at her inner strength and fortitude.

Before he could tell her so, though, Wendy held up her hand like a stop sign. "No pity. Please. I like being independent. It suits me. Besides, I would never want to pass this on to a child." She pushed to her feet, tossing the remnants of her latte away. "Let's go."

"I thought we were going to get a bite to eat."

"I'm not hungry anymore."

Right. Okay. Signal received and understood. Back off.

He tossed his empty cup in the trash as well, then followed her out. It had been so long, too long, since he'd been this attracted to a woman, since he'd even allowed anyone that close. To say he'd been gun-shy after Nikki would be an understatement. But in a different universe, he had the sneaking feeling he and Wendy might've been pretty darned perfect for each other.

In another life, in a less complicated scenario.

As it was, he wasn't sure how to handle this thing with her.

He just knew he wanted to keep seeing her, in whatever way she'd let him.

Outside again, Wendy seemed to relax a bit, her rigid posture easing. He was glad, thinking maybe he hadn't blown this whole thing after all. He and Nikki had been much too young, driven by his hormones and not logic. They hadn't considered the things that were really important, things like compatibility, compassion, camaraderie.

He and Nikki hadn't had anything in common beyond mutual lust.

But the more time he spent with Wendy, Tom began to think that they just might.

If he allowed himself to go down that path. Which was a big unknown.

In the past, he'd only had himself to consider, but now there was Sam too.

Besides, two days and a couple of conversations didn't mean they knew each other that well. It would be silly and ill-advised to fly off on some romantic tangent. He'd been there, done that, with Nikki. Wasn't going there again, thanks very much. Still, it was obvious Wendy had connected with his daughter and he wanted to keep that connection going, if nothing else.

And if he and Wendy got closer along the way, he supposed that wouldn't be so terrible. They'd take it slowly, keep it platonic.

Then he looked at Wendy again, her black hair shining in the sun, and his foolish heart thought this was a person who could make him happy. A hand he could hold. A woman he could know from every perspective, and still find more to explore.

He frowned and looked away, swallowing those unwanted emotions. The scent of freshly mown grass filled the air and bright purple scorpion grasses and deep red Indian paint-brushes shot through the planters around them in all directions.

"I'd appreciate it if you didn't tell anyone, about the Huntington's," Wendy said, as they wandered out of downtown and back into a quieter, more residential area again. "I don't share that with many people."

"Of course. Your secret's safe with me." He stared straight ahead, afraid of looking at her again for fear he'd do something stupid, like pull her into his arms and kiss her. He'd been tempted before, back in the hallway at the hospital, after she'd walked out of her sister-in-law's room. God, that whole situation now made so much more sense—her anxiety, the yearning he'd seen on Wendy's face when she'd held her nephew. He cleared his throat. "Thank you for sharing it with me. It can't have been easy, but, like I said, I'm here if you ever need to talk about it."

She smiled, her dark eyes warming.

This was crazy. This was *so* not him, diving in headfirst, consequences be damned. He'd learned his lesson well with Nikki and had the scars to prove it. It all seemed impossible, yet here he was, about to not let that get in the way of sweeping this woman he barely knew off her feet.

No. He couldn't. He wouldn't jeopardize the only strong connection Sam had made here in Anchorage for a brief fling. Because that's all it could be between him and Wendy. His life was too busy, too complicated, too messy right now for anything else.

He couldn't throw all that responsibility aside and live in the moment.

Could he?

Tom spotted a small walking path leading down to a creek and cocked his head in that direction. "C'mon. Let's check this out before we head back. I need a longer break."

At first, Wendy looked confused, then shrugged and followed him. His heart raced with wild, reckless possibilities, wanting a bit more time to get to know her better, a bit more time to explore this chemistry between them, knowing they'd go back to their complicated lives soon enough. Wanting just a bit more time with Wendy, to unravel the fascinating puzzle she presented.

CHAPTER SIX

WENDY TRAILED BEHIND Tom down to a small, secluded creek. The peaks of the Chugach Mountains were visible over the tree line and red-breasted nuthatches sang from a nearby branch.

A sense of intimacy had formed between her and Tom after she'd told him about her mother's disease. And for some weird reason a weight had been lifted off her by sharing it with him. The fact he hadn't raced for the hills afterward was a nice surprise as well.

Tom was a good man. The more she got to know him, the more she could see that.

He was devoted to his daughter, devoted to his work, devoted to his patients.

He'd probably be just as devoted to the woman he loved.

Sadness pierced her chest, before she brushed it away.

That wouldn't be her. She had no business getting romantically involved with Tom Farber. She wasn't what he needed. Couldn't be. Hell, she wasn't even sure she'd be around in ten years. After all, Huntington's symptoms could start anytime between thirty and fifty and her mother had definitely been on the younger side—the disease taking her life at thirty-eight.

Perhaps she was being silly. Perhaps she should go ahead and get her results.

Put an end to all this terror and strife. Put the cards on the table once and for all.

Wendy stumbled over a stone in the path, distracted by her racing thoughts.

Tom reached out to steady her, his bright blue gaze locking with hers, and time seemed to slow. He looked as dazed as she felt. One of his hands held hers while his other slid around her waist. Tentatively he drew her in closer, closer, until his lips brushed hers in a light kiss.

Stunned, Wendy stood still for a moment, taking it all in—the warmth of his firm lips, the pounding of his heart against hers, the taste of coffee on his tongue.

Before she could overthink her actions, she

rose on tiptoe and kissed him back. He hugged her tighter and she couldn't resist sliding her hands down his muscular back as he deepened the kiss. Tom groaned low, the sound vibrating in her mouth.

They stood near the edge of an ivy umbrella stretching from the cement footing of a footbridge to the trunk of a tree. The scent of honeysuckle filled her lungs and the sweetness of it all made her toes curl.

"Get a room!" a passing canoeist on the creek shouted, laughing.

They broke apart, panting, neither saying a word.

Wendy felt blindsided, astonished, awake for the first time in years.

"Sorry," Tom whispered, his gaze still focused on her lips. "I didn't… I don't…"

They walked back uphill, Tom holding her hand this time.

Things with him felt nice, companionable and so far out of Wendy's comfort zone she had no idea what to do from here. She was used to casual hook-ups, not postcard moments.

They walked back to the hospital where her

car was parked, the odd silence like a third wheel between them. She kept sneaking glances Tom's way, trying to gauge his reaction, but his expression was unreadable.

As they entered Anchorage Mercy again, they separated, in professional territory now. Two elevators opened, and Wendy made for the closest one, along with the rest of the waiting patrons. Tom held her back, however, shaking his head and glancing at the second, empty option. She raised her brows then marched into that one with him. As the doors snapped shut, he kissed her again, all tenderness gone now in favor of passionate intensity. His hands were everywhere—her hips, her leg, the nape of her neck as his lips claimed hers.

The elevator stopped with an abrupt jolt on the next floor, forcing them apart.

Wendy tried to look nonchalant as more nurses and doctors and visitors piled on. Tom's phone buzzed in his pocket and he pulled it out, his somber expression telling her something was off.

"Everything okay?" she asked. "Is it Sam?"

"Everything's fine." His clipped words,

though, reflected the exact opposite. "Just the school, letting me know they appreciated my generous donation to the booster fund." He shoved the phone back into his pocket and stared straight ahead. "She's my top priority these days. I don't want anything to hurt her again."

Right. The reminder was like a bucket of ice water poured over Wendy's head.

His daughter was the only reason she was spending all this time with Tom. The sooner she remembered that, the better. She'd agreed to help him. That was all. Once Sam had settled into her new life, this would all be over, then she could get back to normal.

Because that's what she wanted.

Wasn't it?

The sexual tension sizzling between them cooled as they walked back into Aiyana's room and her sister-in-law gave them each an appraising look. Wendy's lips still tingled from Tom's kisses and she wondered if she looked as guilty as she felt.

"What have you two been doing?" Aiyana asked, the baby in her arms alert and curious.

She shifted the little boy from one arm to the other, then began breastfeeding her tiny daughter. The room filled with the sounds of sucking and breathing, a steady beat, with little gulps in between.

Wendy ignored her question and sat on the edge of the bed. "Where's Ned?"

"He went out to get some food. I was craving sushi."

Tom walked past and squeezed Wendy's shoulder, the gesture making Aiyana's brows rise. Her sister-in-law mouthed, "Oh, my God."

And Wendy mouthed back, "It's nothing."

Except, deep down, it didn't feel like nothing.

In fact, it felt like this *nothing* might just turn out to be *something* after all. And that alone made Wendy want to turn tail and run. Of course, Ned had to walk in with bags of food then and block her exit.

"Where's my sushi?" Aiyana asked, staring at the two containers of California rolls Ned had set on her lap. "That's not sushi."

"Yes, it is," Ned said.

"Nah. Sashimi...now, *that's* sushi." She bit her lip, staring longingly at the raw salmon in her husband's container, then at Tom. "I can finally eat sashimi again, can't I?"

Tom gave Ned an apologetic look. "Yes. It's fine once you're breastfeeding, as long as it's from a reputable place."

Ned sighed then held out his box to her. "Want to trade?"

Aiyana gave him a closed-mouth smile. "No, go ahead, *paipiirak*. It's fine. But next time get me some too, okay?"

"Okay, *uuman*." Ned blew her a kiss.

Wendy held her niece and Tom took the little boy while the new parents dug into their meal with gusto.

"You guys want some?" Ned nudged Tom's arm and offered him a California roll.

He shook his head, though Wendy would've sworn she heard his stomach rumble.

More guilt set in. He had mentioned grabbing a bite to eat earlier.

"No, thanks." Tom cooed over and cuddled her nephew for a few minutes. Seeing him hold the baby made the dormant maternal part of Wendy go all soft and gooey again. She bent to kiss the little girl in her arms. She smelled like freshness and perfection, and Wendy traced one downy cheek with her finger. At times like this she missed her mother most, remembering the nights she'd comforted Wendy after she'd had nightmares. The times she'd patch up her scrapes and bruises from her Little League games. The stories and books they'd read together. *Little Women* had been her mother's favorite.

Ned and Aiyana finished their meal and reluctantly Wendy put her niece back in her bassinet. "I should go. Errands to run and stuff to do." She said her goodbyes, hugging her sister-in-law and her brother. "Call me if you need anything."

"Will do, sis," Ned said. "Thanks again for coming."

Tom waited for her by the door, and a new twinge of anxiety welled inside Wendy. The kisses they'd shared by the creek and in the elevator had been wonderful, but anything more would be a mistake. By the time they left the building and stood outside on the plaza, she knew the wise thing would be to forget about what had happened between her and Tom and take some time to get her head screwed back on straight before she did something foolish. Or more foolish. Ugh. Emotions were feral beasts and she didn't like to need anyone. She'd worked hard to be self-reliant and didn't want to jeopardize that, no matter how she might enjoy getting to know him better.

"Listen, I'm sorry but I think we should just forget about…you know," she said.

"No. I don't." He wasn't going to give her an easy out, apparently. "You mean the kisses?"

People rushed past them, taking no notice of their conversation.

"Yes." She squinted up at him. "And me helping you with Sam. I don't think it's such a great idea. You know, with everything that's going on with me."

"I understand. I do. But I really need—" The vibrating of Tom's phone interrupted him. Cursing under his breath, he pulled it out and frowned. "Shoot. Sorry. I need to go. Another delivery." He started to back away. "This conversation isn't over yet, though. I'll be in touch."

* * *

The following Tuesday night, Tom was home late again, well after six.

He carried the bags of hamburgers and fries he'd picked up after his shift to the kitchen table, said goodbye to the nanny, then took a deep breath before calling out to Sam, "Dinner's ready."

Sam shuffled out of her bedroom and flopped into a chair, her sullen expression matching his mood to a T. Still, he forced a smile and got busy getting plates and napkins for them. This was important. He still needed to discuss what had happened at the school the previous week with his daughter and make sure nothing like that happened again in the future. He also hoped to take Wendy's advice and perhaps begin to bridge the gap between him and Sam. Have a real talk *with* her, instead of the talking *at* each other they usually did.

He'd sat in on Sam's therapy appointment this afternoon as well. The counselor had invited him, and he'd attended with such high expectations, but it hadn't gone as well as he'd hoped. He'd tried his best to remain a silent observer, but when Sam had started talking about her time in Boston and the things Nikki had done in front of their daughter—drugs, partying—it made his blood boil.

If he'd had any idea that stuff had been going on, the danger Nikki had put Sam in, he would've been on a plane back to the East Coast so fast heads would've spun. As it was, picturing Sam cowering alone in her bedroom, door locked and huddled in the corner, afraid one of his ex-wife's loser friends might burst in at any moment and do God knew what...

Those words still hung over him like a storm cloud.

He'd been wrong to leave Boston all those years ago, but he'd had no choice then and he couldn't go back and change things. All he could do now was be better going forward.

He sighed and carried the plates over to the table.

I've been wrong about so many things...

Including what had happened with Wendy last week.

Those kisses, so hot, so sweet, so wrong.

She might well have a horrible, rare genetic

disease that could kill her. He couldn't take that on.

Could I?

After Sam's counseling appointment earlier, he'd done some research on Huntington's disease in his office. It was considered a "late" onset disease, with symptoms first appearing in patients between thirty and fifty—unsteady gait, jerky movements, loss of speech and cognitive abilities, until the body stopped functioning entirely and the poor person withered away and died. Its insidious progress slowly killed its victim's brain cells, many people not realizing what was happening until it was too late.

The fact a young Wendy had had to watch her own mother go through that was unimaginable. The fact an adult Wendy had chosen to get tested then had never found out her results was unfathomable to a control freak like him. As a father, Tom couldn't imagine leaving something like that to chance. With Sam in his life again, he would take every precaution to protect her, even if that meant facing his own mortality.

But he couldn't judge Wendy for her choices,

for keeping her emotional distance from everyone and everything. She'd faced those demons firsthand and didn't want to subject anyone she cared about to them ever again.

Except she let you in, at least a little...

And now that he had his toe in the door, Tom found he didn't want to leave.

She set all his protective instincts and control issues on high alert.

Not that he would ever overstep her boundaries, but the way she'd responded to his kiss told him she felt this strong attraction between them too, even if she refused to act on it. She was probably right. The wise thing to do would be to walk away.

Ugh. It was all so frustrating. He was a problem-solver, a thinker and a fixer. And yet he couldn't seem to sort out his own emotions. So he sucked it up and toughed it out, because that was what he did.

"I learned a lot, sitting in on your session today," he said to Sam by way of easing into their talk, passing her a plate and napkin.

She grunted, didn't even look at him, just futzed with the stuff in her bag.

He sat down and got his own food out before continuing. Never mind the ache in his chest, the yearning to have his daughter look at him with something other than disdain or boredom. Best to dive right in and get the worst over with.

"Sam, about what happened at the school last week—" he started.

"I said I was sorry, okay?" She crumpled up her napkin in her fist. "I told you the stuff I took was going to get thrown away anyway. What? I should have let that fox die instead?"

Her Boston accent got heavier when she was upset. Tom found it endearing beyond belief but didn't think mentioning it now would win him any points. "No. But you should've asked permission. Those are the rules."

She snorted and rolled her eyes. "Rules. That's all you care about."

"Wrong. I care about you too, Sam." He clasped his hands on the table to resist the urge to fold his paper bag into a neat square. "How about we put that behind us? I'd much rather discuss your therapy appointment today. I had no idea about the stuff you dealt with back in

Boston. What you saw. I want you to know I'll always be here to protect you, okay? If you ever feel scared or sad or unsure or whatever, you come to me. You'll always have a safe place here. I know you don't think I want you in my life, but nothing could be further from the truth."

She looked up at him, held his gaze for a moment before sighing and glancing away. "Okay."

Perhaps Wendy had been right. Perhaps just being there for her would open up all sorts of new doorways. Encouraged, he continued on with another idea he'd had this afternoon. "I thought maybe we could go shopping for some new clothes before your trip to Fairbanks in a few weeks."

Sam shoved a couple of fries in her mouth and glared at him while she chewed. "Why? I probably won't leave their house anyway. You don't like the same things I do, so let's not."

Yeah, this part of the conversation was going about as well as he'd expected. Clothes shopping was a no-go. It had been a dumb idea in the first place and he had to admit a bit of relief on that one. He'd only offered because he thought she might like it and not because he enjoyed hanging out at the mall. He changed the subject. "So, Wendy's great. I'm glad you two got to know each other."

Sam said something incoherent around her bite of burger.

"The counselor said today maybe you should get involved in some kind of after-school activity. Anything in particular you'd like to do? Drama club? Sports?"

"I don't know," Sam said, her tone flat. "I like reading."

"Anchorage has a great library. Maybe you could volunteer there?"

Sam stared at him while she chewed. "Maybe."

"Did I tell you Wendy and I had coffee last week, after you left the hospital?"

Finally, she expressed a different emotion other than boredom. Outrage.

Not what he was going for.

"Seriously?" Sam's cheeks flushed, and her eyes glittered with tears. Tom hadn't told her that to upset her, but it seemed he'd done just that. "You just don't stop, do you?"

"What?" He honestly had no clue. "We didn't really discuss anything about you, I promise."

"Don't act like you care about me. It's just more control for you, isn't it? You hate the fact that Wendy and I are friends now and we talk about stuff you'll never know, don't you?"

"*Hate*'s a strong word and you throw it around a lot." Tom forced himself to take a bite of his burger, though he could've been chewing cardboard for all he tasted it. "It was nothing, I swear. I wasn't trying to go behind your back, Sam. You and Wendy have a lot in common. I'm glad you've got someone to talk to."

Sam harrumphed and devoured more of her food.

"Maybe we could have lunch too sometimes, if I'm not busy with a patient." When he didn't get a response, he kept talking, hoping to open some new avenues of discussion between them. "I remember when we first moved into the apartment back in Boston, your mom and I used to have lunch sometimes at this little falafel place down the street. I'm not sure it's there anymore. I think it was called Shawarma

King, or something. Real hole-in-the-wall, but the best hummus—"

"God, you're doing it again!" Sam pushed to her feet and shoved the rest of her food back in her bag before carrying it away to her room. "Just stop pushing me! I don't want to talk about Mom and I don't want to have lunch with you, okay? Stay away from Wendy. I've got homework to do."

After her door closed, Tom had sat there at the table, finishing his burger and fries alone, the news droning in the background, depressing as usual.

Man, he was so bad at all this. Why was he so bad at this?

It was embarrassing. It was sad. It was soul-crushing.

Feeling both tired and restless, Tom discarded his trash, then watched some TV, flipping through the channels for hours but never settling on anything too long. He listened for sounds from Sam's room, imagined her opening up her bedroom door and coming out to sit with him, but no. Contemplated going to her door and begging her to come out, but that didn't seem right either.

Finally, he gave up and shut off the lights, then walked down the hall to his own bedroom, the smooth hardwood floors cool beneath his bare feet, the air-conditioning maintaining the perfect temperature, his two-bedroom apartment decorated to spartan perfection, everything chosen for comfort or usefulness.

Yet his home no longer brought him the welcoming serenity it once had.

Despite doing his best to follow Wendy's advice, his daughter hadn't said more than a handful of words to him. His heart ached at the fact nothing he tried on his own seemed to make any difference with Sam. Tom was forced to give in to the cold, hard truth.

He couldn't do this by himself.

The counseling helped Sam, but he needed some support too. He needed Wendy, despite his daughter's wishes to the contrary.

Tom stopped partway down the hall and headed back to the kitchen, where Sam had stuck Wendy's business card to the fridge with a magnet. A glance at the clock showed it was now a few minutes after 11 p.m. Late, yes, but desperate times called for desperate measures.

And he *had* told Wendy he'd be in touch.

Tom grabbed his cellphone from the charger and dialed.

After a few rings a husky female voice answered, "Hello?"

Great, he'd woken her up. He cleared his throat. "Hi. It's Tom."

"What's wrong?" Wendy said, her tone groggy. "Did something happen to Sam?"

"No, she's fine." The knot between his shoulder blades eased at the sound of her voice and Tom continued down the hall and into his bedroom, shutting the door behind him. "I wanted to talk to you."

Silence.

"Hello?" Tom asked.

Wendy moaned, low and sultry. And just like that, their kiss flashed back into his head. The feel of her hand in his, the sweet smell of her floral perfume, the taste of coffee and passion on her tongue. More images flooded in—Wendy, entwined in his sheets as he nuzzled and licked her all over, making her cry out his name as he brought her to the brink of climax…

His traitorous body twitched in response.

"Am I interrupting something?" he asked, taking a deep breath to calm his raging libido.

"No," she said, her tone impatient. "What can I do for you?"

A loaded question if ever there was one.

Frustrated in more ways than one, Tom scrubbed his hand over his face.

He shifted his stance, reminding himself that Wendy Smith was not the woman for him. Things were too complicated. He needed her help to fix things between him and Sam. His daughter needed to be his top priority. His only priority, no matter what his body was urging to the contrary.

Tom pressed on.

"I called to talk about Sam. I know the counselor's returned from vacation and all, but if you wanted to keep meeting my daughter in the cafeteria, as a friend, I'd be fine with that." He rubbed his eyes. "Look, the truth is I'm afraid I'm going to screw all this up without you, to be honest. Tonight I brought up what happened with her at school last week and I tried to do the things you mentioned—reassuring her about the weekend with my parents, asking her about her day, opening up and engaging with her—but they're not working."

Wendy sighed. "You know you're putting me in a tough spot."

"I know, but I'm desperate. I do my best to give my daughter as much time as possible, but I have to work to support us both. Her private school is expensive." Tom sighed and shook his head. "I'm out of ideas here. What do you suggest I do? The counselor mentioned getting her involved in some extracurricular activities. She mentioned she likes reading. I thought maybe she could volunteer at the local library, but I'm not sure how we'd work that out logistics-wise, now that I think about it. With the nanny and my schedule and—"

"Calm down," Wendy said. "I may have another solution. Did you know we were putting in a new family lounge in the ER?"

"No."

"It was Jake's idea. It'll be geared toward relaxing the kids who come in while their parents are being treated. We set up a special room with video games, toys, computers to do their homework, a television and a kid-friendly library with everything from picture books to young adult novels. The ER staff planned to take turns on our breaks reading to the kids, but maybe Sam would enjoy taking over for the little ones in the afternoon."

"Wow. Uh..." Sam had told him she liked reading. It sounded like a good fit to him. "Sorry. Yes, I think she'd like that. But then again, she hardly speaks to me. On the rare occasions when she does surprise me with a full sentence, it's usually to tell me how much she hates me, how she knows I don't want her, or how she wishes I'd died instead of her mother."

Those times, he'd rather she'd just stayed quiet.

"I'm sorry," Wendy said, her tone genuine. "She's processing a lot of anger."

"Please say you'll help me," he pleaded. "Whatever she needs. I'll do anything. Please?"

The line was quiet for so long Tom wondered if Wendy was still there. Then she said, "Fine. Let me talk to her about the lounge at lunch tomorrow and see what she says. If it's a yes, then you can come down to the ER around four o'clock on Friday afternoon and hopefully see a different side of Sam. One that'll change your perspective."

Yes! He wouldn't miss this opportunity for the world. "Perfect. Thank you."

"And for goodness' sake, don't mention any of this to her either. Make up some excuse for coming down but leave me out of it." Wendy sighed. "This is a chance to start something new with your daughter. Don't screw it up."

CHAPTER SEVEN

BY THREE O'CLOCK on Thursday afternoon, Tom finished delivering his third baby of the day and was in desperate need of a break. There must have been a full moon or something, from the number of women going into labor. He jotted notes in one of his charts at the nurses' station then squeezed his tired eyes shut, the words blurring from his fatigue.

"I'm going to run down to the cafeteria and grab a protein bar and a bottled water. Want anything?" he asked the nurse at the desk.

"No, thanks," she said. "But you'd better hurry. ER called and said another delivery just arrived downstairs."

"Thanks." They must be going for a record or something. "I'll hurry."

Tom walked down the hall toward the elevators, past the drinking fountain where he and Wendy had almost kissed. Which brought up memories of them walking down by the stream where they had, in fact, kissed.

Dammit. He shouldn't be having those thoughts again. Wendy was helping him with Sam. She wasn't a woman he should get involved with. If things went south between them, he'd be responsible for Sam losing the only person she'd really opened up to here in Anchorage. No. He couldn't risk it. Kissing Wendy down by the stream had been really, really stupid. He hadn't planned it, that was for sure. But, man. That one kiss had lit a wildfire of lust in his blood, blazing white-hot. Thank God, that canoeist had rowed by and interrupted them.

But he had more to think about than himself now. He had Sam.

Tom rode the elevator down to the basement, hugging the corner of the car, fiddling with his phone without really paying attention to what was on the screen. He was too busy convincing himself why taking things further with Wendy was a bad idea.

There was also the fact that when he'd kissed her he'd gotten lost in the moment, had become oblivious to everything else around him. For a control junkie like him that didn't sit well. He couldn't risk losing his common sense, not when things with Sam were so precarious.

Then there was Wendy's family history of Huntington's disease. While he wasn't freaked out by the possibility of it, the fact she'd never gotten her results raised a million red flags for him. He understood being nervous or scared, but the only way to deal with an issue was to face it. Besides, he'd been there, done that with Nikki, had fallen for a woman who'd avoided her problems and it had nearly cost him everything.

No way would he charge headlong into the same situation again.

Not that he was in love with Wendy Smith.

That would be ridiculous. They'd just met. They barely knew each other.

He liked kissing her. He liked talking to her.

They were friends. She was helping him with Sam. That was all.

The elevator doors slid open and Tom walked out into the brightly lit basement hallway. This far past the noon hour, the lunch crowds had thinned out, which was good. He checked his watch then headed into the cafeteria, cruising through the display cases filled with goodies and the restocked shelves of prepackaged sandwiches and chips and cookies. The air smelled of garlic and melted cheese and if he'd had longer he would've liked to eat something more substantial than a protein bar, but time was of the essence. He expected his phone to alert him anytime now to the new delivery arrival from the ER.

He grabbed a protein bar from the rack and a bottled water from the refrigerated case, then strode over to the cashier to pay for them. As he waited in line, conversation buzzed around him. Behind where he stood was a row of artificial plants, blocking off the dining area from the food service area. Booths were on the other side.

The cashier handed him his change and he halted halfway through stowing his wallet away in the back pocket of his scrubs, hearing Sam's laugh.

His chest squeezed. It had been a long time since he'd heard that sound.

She and Wendy must be having their chat in

one of the booths nearby. He flashed the cashier a grateful smile then moved out of the way of the other patrons waiting behind him. He hated eavesdropping, but he couldn't seem to stop himself. His heart ached to know more about his daughter, especially after the counseling appointment he'd sat in on yesterday.

Tom didn't mean to push her. He didn't. He was trying, but he felt like a blind man in a maze most of the time. He tore open the wrapper of his protein bar and nibbled on it while he leaned against the half wall below the line of plants.

"Seriously, though, I know how you feel," he heard Wendy say. "I was the same way after my mom died."

"How old were you again?" Sam asked.

"Ten."

"That sucks."

"Yeah. It was pretty scary, seeing her rapid decline, health-wise. I was too young to understand all of it."

"Did you get to say goodbye?"

"Sort of. My dad took me up to her hospital room that last night. She was in a coma by that point, but the nurses all said she could still hear us."

Sam didn't say anything for a moment, seemingly thinking that over. "I didn't have that. I never really got to say goodbye. My mom went to sleep and never woke up. Toward the end, I used to take care of her, like I was the mom or something. Social Services would make these surprise visits and I didn't want to get taken away and put in foster care, so I did what I had to do to make it look like everything was fine, even though it wasn't. It really, really wasn't."

Tom's heart went into free fall even though the social workers he'd spoken to when he'd picked up Sam in Boston had filled him in on the basic details. The pain in his daughter's voice was unfathomable. Pain like that left scars. Deep ones. He felt gutted.

Sam gave a sad little snort. "She died at a party one night at one of her friend's houses. Overdosed. I didn't find out until the next morning when the police showed up with a social worker to take me into child protective services. They didn't have to tell me she was dead.

I knew right away, just from the looks on their faces." His daughter's voice grew quieter now, hollower. "I never got a chance to say goodbye."

"Oh, sweetie," Wendy said. "I'm so, so sorry."

"Do you still think about your mom?" Sam asked after a moment.

"I do," Wendy said. "Every day."

Tom's throat tightened.

"Some days I'm so sad I don't want to get out of bed." Sam's words were brittle. "All I want is my mom, and I have to go to school and Dad's there expecting me to be all normal and stuff, and it just seems so stupid. I'd give anything for just one more day with my mom. No matter what she did or how bad she was."

His daughter's voice broke and through the leaves of the plants Tom saw Wendy move to the other side of the booth to put her arm around Sam.

"I'm sorry, sweetie," she said. Nothing else, just that. She stroked Sam's hair and rested her chin atop his daughter's head, letting her cry it out.

"I know it's dumb and I should get over it." Sam sniffled. "It's been more than a year."

"Listen, sweetie. You take all the time you need. Everybody's grief is different," Wendy said. "You never really get over it. You just learn to deal with it better and eventually it doesn't hurt so bad and you can get back to life and enjoy things again. She'll still be with you, in your heart. We're both lucky too. We have family that love us and are there for us." Grateful warmth spread through Tom at her inclusion of him. "Doing regular stuff actually helps too. Getting out of bed. Going to school. It's sort of fake it till you make it. Act normal and pretty soon all that sadness inside you eases. You can think of your mom and remember happy things. It gets easier."

"That's what my dad says too," Sam said after a minute, her voice a bit rough from crying. "But I'm scared of losing him now too. What if he goes to work one day and never comes back?"

"Oh, honey." Tom heard tears in Wendy's voice too. "Your dad's healthy and he's going to be here a long, long time to take care of you. Maybe you should talk this out with him. Tell him how you feel."

There was a rustle of fabric as Sam shrugged. "Yeah, maybe. He gets kinda sappy when we talk about mushy stuff like that, though."

"He does, huh?"

"Yes." He could just imagine the eye roll that went with that admission. Funny, but this time it made him smile. "But it's sort of sweet, I suppose. Don't tell him I said that, though."

"Promise." There was a smile in Wendy's voice.

"I just… I feel like a pain in his butt most of the time. He's always so perfect and the apartment is so clean and spotless," his daughter said. "It makes me miss home even more. I miss my old room."

Pain stabbed Tom's chest. Why hadn't Sam told *him* that? If she wanted her room redone, he'd be fine with that. Whatever it took to make her happy. All she had to do was ask. Why hadn't she asked?

Maybe because you didn't let her…

"Do you ever talk to her?" Sam asked. "Your mom, I mean. The counselor says it might help me."

"Sure," Wendy said. "I talk to my mom sometimes."

"Does she ever answer?" Sam sighed. "Not like literally or anything. But do you ever feel she's with you or something?"

Wendy went quiet. Tom lived and died in those few seconds. He doubted she'd told Sam about her mother's Huntington's disease. Knowing how Wendy felt about getting her test results, that question must've hit her like a sledgehammer.

"Yeah, I do," Wendy said at last, her tone a bit strained. "How about you?"

"I feel her with me, yeah. I don't say anything to Dad, though. He and Mom really didn't get along. I tried to ask her about him lots of times, but all she'd tell me was bad stuff about him." Sam took a deep breath. "Can I tell you another secret?"

"Of course," Wendy said. "You can tell me anything, sweetie."

"I never believed he was as bad as Mom said. Now that I live with him, I know he's not. He tries, too hard mostly, but he's a guy and they're weird."

"Definitely weird." The smile returned to Wendy's voice, and Tom found himself grinning too, astonished by his daughter's admission that he wasn't a monster after all.

Through the leaves, he saw Sam yank a napkin from the dispenser on the table then blow her nose.

"Maybe you should try going easier on your dad," Wendy said. "I mean, it's your call and definitely talk to your counselor about it first. I don't know him as well as you, but he seems like he genuinely wants to help. Maybe share with him some of the stuff you told me too. I won't say a word to him, I promise, but I bet he'd love to have these kinds of talks with you."

Tom did. So much it hurt.

"Yeah, maybe. I don't know. It's hard."

"Everything worthwhile in life is hard."

"I guess." Sam yawned. "I should get back to Dad's office. The nanny will be there soon. What time do you want me down in the ER tomorrow?"

Sounds of movement echoed through the plants and Tom took that as his cue to leave. The last thing he needed was to get busted listening in on his daughter's chats with Wendy. Even though he couldn't bring himself to regret his eavesdropping. He was still a bit stunned to hear that maybe, just maybe, his daughter didn't loathe him after all.

He'd made it nearly to the exit when Wendy called from behind him. "Tom?"

Damn. So close. He forced what he hoped was an innocent smile and turned. "Hey. I'm in between deliveries, so I made a quick run down here for sustenance. I forgot you'd be here. Hey, Sam."

He managed not to cringe at his own nervous babbling, barely.

His daughter mumbled hello under her breath, her gaze lowered.

"Are you guys heading back?" he asked as they walked over to him. "We can ride up together."

They walked through the hallway, the slight buzz of the fluorescent lights above and the distant hum of a floor buffer the only noises. Tom held the elevator doors for them, then pushed the buttons for the ER and L&D. Wendy's ponytail brushed his arm as the elevator jolted upward and the scent of her floral shampoo enveloped him.

The elevator stopped on the first floor and the doors opened. Sam got off, turning to give them a small wave. "Going back to Dad's office." To his shock and amazement, she glanced his way and gave him a tiny ghost of a smile. "See you at home."

Wendy started out after her, but Tom caught her arm. "Uh, can you come upstairs with me for a sec? I've got something I'd like your opinion on."

She raised a brow but stepped back inside the elevator just the same.

No sooner had the doors shut than he was kissing her again. She was as surprised as he was, if the tiny squeak that came out of her was any indication. It was just that he felt so joyful and grateful and her lips were soft and warm beneath his and he cupped her cheeks, his thumbs stroking her smooth skin. Those warning bells in his head sounded again, telling him how dangerous this was, but then she kissed him back, hot and deep and wonderful.

His heart inched a bit more past "like" and into "more" territory...

Ding!

The elevator doors opened on the L&D floor and they pulled apart. Tom stepped back, feeling blurry and slow and a bit stunned at the depth of emotion swirling inside him for this woman who'd just worked a small miracle on his behalf.

"You didn't really need my opinion on that, did you?" she whispered.

"No," he said, his voice huskier than usual. "Uh, thanks again for spending time with Sam."

"You're welcome." Wendy swallowed hard and moved out into the hallway, heading for the stairwell. "I...um...need to get back to the ER."

"Okay."

"Tomorrow. Four p.m."

"I'll be there."

She walked away, stopping to glance back at him. And because he didn't know what to say, he just looked at her, all those pretty curves and silky hair and her smile.

Then she pushed through the door to the stairwell and disappeared, and Tom leaned against the wall, his phone buzzing in the front pocket of his scrub shirt, wondering exactly what the hell he was doing, falling for the one woman who should be totally off-limits.

CHAPTER EIGHT

"How's things?" Jake asked Wendy late Friday morning as he stood over her desk in the ER. "Everything ready for the opening of the Family Lounge?"

"Yep." She continued to work on the chart in front of her, not meeting his gaze. "Good to go. Got a special reader for this afternoon. How are things with you?"

"Fine. Fine. Just finished lancing a boil in Trauma Bay Two, so I can't complain," he said, his words dripping with sarcasm. "I'm taking Molly out to dinner at Ursa again tonight."

"Nice. Hopefully it'll go better than last time you guys went there."

"Right." Jake snorted. A baby cried in the waiting room down the hall. "What about you? Got plans for tonight?"

"I'm here for another eight hours at least, buddy." For a moment, Wendy wondered what Tom was doing, but quickly shoved those thoughts aside. It was the fatigue. Had to be. Of course, that was Tom's fault too, seeing as how she wasn't sleeping well, reliving those steamy kisses in the elevator with him the previous day each time she closed her eyes, unable to get him out of her head. Truth was, each time she saw him the staunch barriers around her heart crumbled a bit more. Soon they'd be gone completely and then what would she do?

Fall head over heels for him, that's what...

Irritated, she finished documenting in the chart she was working on, then dropped it into her outgoing box for transport back to Medical Records. Someday they'd go fully digital at Anchorage Mercy, but today was not that day. She slid off her stool ready to grab the next patient file. "Have fun tonight."

Jake continued. "So Ned and Aiyana had their twins?"

"Yep." She stopped and looked back at him. "Cute kids. You should stop by their house and see them. Would be good practice for when you and Molly have your own."

"True," he said, closing the file in front of

him before going for her jugular. The guy was her best friend, but subtlety wasn't his forte. "What about you?"

She sighed and walked back to her desk. "What about me?"

"Kids."

"Look, buddy. You know my stance on that. Fine for other people, not for me."

"Because of the HD."

"Bingo."

Jake didn't even blink as he dropped another bombshell. "Does Tom know?"

"Excuse me?" Wendy glanced around then took his arm and pulled him aside. "What the hell are you talking about?"

"I might have heard a few things. Rumors about the two of you." He shrugged.

"Well, you can just un-hear them." She kept her voice low, not wanting to start any more gossip circulating. "There's nothing going on between Tom Farber and me, okay?"

"Uh-huh." Jake leaned a shoulder against the wall, giving her a skeptical look. "I've got eyes, you know. I've seen the two of you talking.

Don't think I haven't noticed how you get all doe-eyed and moony whenever he's around."

"Moony? It that even a word?" Wendy scrunched her nose, desperate to end this discussion as quickly as possible. She held up a hand to stop him from answering. "It doesn't matter. I know you mean well, but there's nothing between us, okay?"

"Why not? He's available. You're available." Jake raised a brow at her.

"Because I'm not looking to have a relationship with anyone right now. We're friends. I'm helping him out with his daughter. That's it." *Liar.*

"Fine, but it's clear you like him," Jake said, hitting a bit too close to home for Wendy's comfort. And darn if he wasn't right too. If she was honest, she *way more* than liked Tom at this point and that was a problem. "True love isn't always easy to recognize is all I'm saying. Look at Molly and me. We were at loggerheads over Bobby's case for weeks until one night— *boom!*"

Except she didn't love Tom Farber.
Do I?

Jake bent to catch her eye and snickered. "Yep, there it is again. The moony look."

No. Enough. She grabbed the next chart in the pile and turned away. "You keep pestering me about this and you'll get a moon all right, just not the one you're expecting. Remember that time in high school, after the football game, when I mooned the opposing team?"

"How can I forget?" Jake gave her a flat look. "You photobombed my parents' picture with your butt."

She bit her lip to keep from laughing. "Yeah, I did. Still sorry about that, buddy." She walked back over and patted him on the back. "I know you mean well, Jake. But please mind your own business."

"Tom's a good guy, in case you were wondering," he said. "I've worked a couple of cases with him. He's smart and conscientious and kind. Everybody likes him."

"Which part of mind your own business didn't you understand?" She crossed her arms knowing her best bud wouldn't stop until she gave him something. "Like I said, he and I are...*friends*. That's it." Jake gave that skeptical stare again. "Fine. We may have kissed a few times, but seriously? Look, think of it like having a winning lottery ticket, but instead of jinxing it you'd rather book a trip to Florida and tell people you're having bunion surgery to throw them off the trail."

Jake scowled. "That's a lot of mixed metaphors. Did you just compare Tom to bunions?"

"What?" Wendy thought back over her words and had a hard time keeping them straight. Fitting, since she had the same problem with her feelings for Tom. "No. I don't know. Oh, just forget it. I don't even know why I'm telling you any of this."

"Because—" Jake's tone went quiet and sincere "—we're friends and I want you to be happy and not die alone with a million cats."

"I have one cat. Dot."

With a sigh, she headed toward the waiting room to call back the next patient, only to stop when a call came in over the radio. EMT Zac Taylor's voice echoed through the air. "Pregnant teen in labor. Found alone near Bicentennial Park. Already crowning. No identification. No prenatal care. Unsure of gestation but estimated to be around thirty-three weeks. Mother appears slightly cyanotic. Breathing irregular. En route to Anchorage Mercy ER."

"Damn." Instead of calling back the patient, Wendy returned the chart to the rack then grabbed a gown and mask off the nearby shelf and followed Jake to the ambulance entrance. "Should we call Respiratory Therapy down for a consult?"

"Yep," Jake said, tying his gown behind his neck. "And OB. Better safe than sorry."

Wendy did as he requested then finished suiting up as the automatic doors swished open and the paramedic crew rushed into the ER with a screaming young girl on a stretcher. Zac gave them the rundown again as they headed for Trauma Bay One.

"Get an incubator in here, please," Jake called as he examined the patient. The young girl had short black hair and looked fifteen or sixteen. The ambulance crew had stripped her from the waist down and covered her with a white sheet. She writhed on the gurney. Once they got the patient transferred to a hospital bed in the trauma bay, Wendy did her best to reassure the girl while Jake examined her.

The girl cried out, "It hurts."

Wendy set up the incubator then hurried to take the girl's hand, noting a slight blue tinge around the girl's lips. "Just breathe, honey. In and out." She demonstrated. "Do it with me."

The girl looked up, her eyes filled with tears, face red, her expression a mix of pain and fear. "I can't do this."

"You can, and you will." Wendy looked up as Tom entered the room. He was the OB on call again today. She gave him a brief nod then refocused on the patient. "Squeeze my hand as hard as you can. You won't hurt me."

Tom shrugged into a fresh gown, moving in beside Jake. "I can take over."

"Here comes another one," the girl cried out, squeezing Wendy's hand hard.

Jake finished checking the patient's vitals then stepped away. "All yours, Dr. Farber. I've got a backlog of people waiting before my shift ends. Thanks." He gave Wendy a pointed look as he left the trauma bay.

Tom nodded to the teenaged girl. "Bear down and push."

"Yes! Just like that. You're doing great." When the contraction ended Wendy used the corner of the sheet to blot the sweat from the girl's forehead and upper lip. "I'm Wendy, the nurse who'll help you through this. What's your name?"

"Amber," the girl panted.

"Is there someone we can call for you, Amber?" Wendy asked. "Family member? Friend?"

"No. No one. Please. They don't know. No one knows. Oh, God. Not again," she cried.

"You're doing great," Wendy said, trying to bolster the girl's strength with her own.

"One more push should do it, Amber," Tom called from the end of the bed.

After the contraction, Amber flopped back on the bed, exhausted, her eyes pleading. "Promise me it'll be okay."

Wendy looked up and caught Tom's too-perceptive gaze.

"We'll do our best, Amber, I promise," she said.

The girl loosened her grip and Wendy stepped away to check the monitors.

"Wait." Tom frowned down between the patient's legs. "Don't push."

"What's wrong?" Amber asked, frantic.

Wendy moved in beside Tom to see what was happening.

"The cord is wrapped around the baby's neck," he whispered, then gave the patient a reassuring smile. "Don't. Push."

After a few tense minutes Tom looked up at Wendy, relief etched on his handsome face. "Okay, good to go. On the next contraction, Amber, I want you to push out your baby."

In no time a squirming newborn girl entered the world with a tiny cry of displeasure. The cord was cut and Wendy took the tiny baby, wrapping her in a towel. She did a quick assessment then turned to Amber. "Want to see her?"

"Chest...hurts." The girl struggled for breath, the bluish color of her lips increasing. "Can't... breathe."

"Get a crash cart in here now!" Wendy yelled to the residents, holding the infant close.

"Where's Respiratory Therapy?" Tom leaned

out past the curtains surrounding the trauma bay then looked back at Wendy. "Stabilize that infant while we take care of the mom."

"No pulse." A resident sidled into Wendy's place near the head of Amber's bed as the heart monitor flatlined. "Initiating CPR."

The resident began chest compressions while another nurse placed an oxygen mask over the patient's face. The team from Respiratory Therapy arrived along with the pulmonologist on call.

Tom stepped back. "Get the paddles ready."

As he gave the lung specialist the rundown on the delivery, Wendy raced through the curtains and headed across the hall. Her mind clicked into auto-nurse mode when she reached the warming table, wiping down the too-quiet newborn to stimulate movement. "I need your weight, little one."

She placed the baby on a small scale—four point one pounds—then counted her heart and respiratory rates. Both normal, thank goodness. She fastened a pulse oximeter to the infant's tiny hand to evaluate her blood oxygen level. The baby flexed her arms and legs, her color pale. Wendy distracted herself by documenting the vitals. Pulse ox ninety. Heart rate one eighty. Increased respiratory effort. Initial Apgar score five.

Tom came in a few moments later, looking grim as he surveyed her notes.

"Let's get an IV line in, then give her a bolus of normal saline and get the baby hooked up to some supplemental oxygen." He inserted a tiny nasal cannula into the infant's nostrils, taping the tubing to her cheeks, then set the flow meter to provide the appropriate level of oxygen. Wendy started an IV in the tiny girl's left arm—noting the baby didn't flinch or cry. Not good. While she taped down the line and immobilized the baby's limb in an extended position, Tom did a quick heel stick to evaluate the infant's blood sugar level.

They worked quickly, quietly and efficiently, like they'd been a team for years.

"Blood glucose twenty-five." He rummaged around a drawer beneath the warmer until he found a reference card for the recommended dosages by weight. "Add a bolus of dextrose."

Wendy filled the syringes and administered the contents via the IV line.

"Come on, baby," she said, rubbing the infant's thighs to perk her up.

The door opened and in walked a nurse from L&D.

"Need help, Tom?" the nurse asked.

"We're managing," he said. "Any openings in the NICU yet?"

"Yep. This little one will be going into room forty-one. The mom's doing better."

Wendy's heart tripped. Even though she'd been working, keeping her emotions well under lock and key, a small part of her had automatically assumed the worst, because…well, that was her experience. People got sick. People died. People didn't get better.

All these years, she'd put her energy into moving forward, moving on. Trying to put the past behind her and live only for the day, because today was sometimes all you had. She'd thought by not knowing her results, she'd escaped. Except she hadn't escaped anything at all. Her mother's death, the disease, was still there, all-pervasive, affecting every aspect of her life because of the barriers she'd built to keep everyone else out.

She leaned back to peer through the glass in the door and spotted the respiratory therapy team leaving the trauma bay where Amber was being kept. The girl looked pale, her eyes wide and wild with fear, but she was alert and breathing, albeit with an oxygen mask. They'd still have to discover what had caused the chest pains and the sudden cardiac arrest, but she was alive. Wendy's grip on the stark future she'd planned for herself slipped a tad.

Maybe things could work out okay. Maybe life didn't have to be black or white.

Maybe there was room for some gray, some hope, some closeness and connection.

"That's fantastic!" Tom said to the nurse. "Best news I've had all day."

His dazzling smile set Wendy's pulse racing once more.

Maybe there was a chance for her and Tom after all.

If they took it slowly, step by step, because she was still more than a little wary of any sort of happily-ever-after.

"Isn't it great, Wendy?" Tom asked, nudging her with his arm.

"Yeah, it's awesome," she said, still feeling a bit dazed despite her duties.

The nurse looked between them then nodded. "You sure you don't need me in here?"

"We've got it, thanks," Tom said. "We'll have the infant ready for transport soon."

"You okay?" he asked Wendy once they were alone again.

"Sure." She'd been a trauma nurse for nearly a decade and was well versed in keeping it professional, even if she was failing a bit at the moment. Hey, having the bedrock of your belief systems rocked like a hurricane could do that to a girl. She shook off her errant thoughts and concentrated on the case once more. "What do you think caused Amber's issues post-delivery?"

He shook his head, his grin turning to a thoughtful expression. "Hard to say at this point, until we get further testing done. Could be a congenital heart defect. Pulmonary embolism. Any number of preexisting conditions can worsen or arise during pregnancy and delivery." He fiddled with the stuff in the warmer drawer, straightening it like he always did when he was stressed. "Now that the crisis is over, we'll need to get a full history and physical on her, blood tests to make sure she wasn't using any drugs or in withdrawal. Try to locate her next of kin, figure out what happens when she and her baby are well enough to go home."

From what she'd heard from Sam the other day and what Tom had told her about his rocky marriage, he had to be thinking about his ex-wife right now. "Amber isn't Nikki."

"No, I know." He closed the drawer and gave her a faint smile that looked so sad she wanted to pull him into her arms and hug him until all his pain disappeared. Tom turned away, though, to look down at their tiniest patient. The newborn wailed on the warming table, and her little arms and legs flailed. "She reminds me of Sam after she was born. So fragile and precious."

"Her color's improving," Wendy noted, moving in beside him. "And she's more alert."

"Heart rate down to one hundred and twenty." He gave Wendy a gentle smile, before examining the increasingly active baby again. "I'd give her a second Apgar score of seven."

Not a perfect ten but improved. Wendy jotted it in the notes, then set the chart aside, placing her hand on Tom's arm. "Sam might have started out at a disadvantage, but she's so lucky to have a father like you. She might seem fragile, but she's stronger than you think. I shouldn't say this, but she told me the other day that you're not as bad as she thought you were."

Tom snorted and placed his hand atop Wendy's as they stood over the baby. "Considering what we've been through these past couple of months, I'm taking that as a compliment."

"You should." Wendy winked then stepped away, assuming her professional nurse persona again. "Orders, Doctor?"

"Right. This patient is stable enough for transport up to the NICU," Tom said, clearing his throat. His voice was a tad rougher than usual. "If you tell the L&D nurse, I'll get the baby situated in the incubator. And thank you, Wendy. For everything."

"You bet." She started for the door, then

stopped and turned back to him. "I'll try to find out more information about Amber's identity and next of kin this afternoon. Looks like RT and Pulmonology are taking over the mother's care from here."

After summoning the other nurse and watching as the baby was wheeled out in the incubator, Wendy assisted the residents with ordering the testing for Amber, then got her registered into the system before sending one of the nursing students to take her history and physical.

By the time that was done, Tom had finished making his notes on the baby's file and was stripping off his soiled gown and shoving it into a biohazard bin. "I'll see you later, then. Four o'clock, right?"

"Right." Wendy nodded. "Family lounge."

He started out of the ER then stopped and turned back, his blue eyes warm. "Thanks again for the help."

He was late. Dammit. It had been a busy morning and an even busier afternoon. By the time Tom was able to get away and head back downstairs it was about four-twenty. He slipped into the room marked "Family Lounge" at the end of the hall and spotted Wendy across the space, busily shelving books and putting away toys. She stopped to chat quietly with a few parents sitting at a table in the back of the room, while Sam held story time to occupy five small kids ranging in age from maybe six all the way down to one year, both boys and girls. They sat in a circle on the floor while she read their selection.

Wendy caught his gaze and motioned for him to be quiet and come stand near her.

Engrossed in her task, Sam didn't seem to notice his arrival as she made an exaggerated honking noise that sent the kids into a fit of giggles.

Tom felt a mix of awe and disbelief as he watched his daughter.

"Welcome to Storytime," Wendy whispered as he moved in beside her. "This helps all of them forget about their troubles for a while." Wendy looked up at him. "Your daughter included."

Sam finished the book and, with a big smile, accepted a round of applause from her audience. Then the circle shifted, as a few of the kids departed with their parents while a couple of new ones arrived, and she began to read again.

"I can't believe it," Tom whispered, his eyes locked on Sam. "She's actually smiling."

"She has a beautiful smile," Wendy pointed out.

"It's been so long, I'd forgotten."

They watched through two more stories before Sam finally looked up and spotted Tom. She finished the book and excused herself to the kids, her grin fading as she walked over to join Wendy and Tom.

"Dad." Sam stopped before them, arms crossed, a defensive pose he was far too familiar with these days. "What are you doing here?"

"Uh, sorry. Didn't mean to interrupt." Tom felt unaccountably nervous. He really wanted this to go well. *Please, God, let this go well.* "I came to check on a case from earlier and saw you reading in here as I passed by."

Wendy gave him a nod and a wink.

Sam's posture relaxed slightly, though her gaze remained wary. "Before you lecture me, my homework's already finished. And you said I should get involved in something after school."

Tom frowned. "Why would I lecture you?"

"Because that's what you always do when I don't follow your rules."

He blinked at his daughter, not sure how to respond. It was like that final argument with Nikki all over again. *"I'm leaving you because I'm sick of living with your rules. You can't control everything, Tom. Get used to it."* He'd thought he was getting better, had tried so hard not to repeat his mistakes, but apparently all of that had gone right out the window when his daughter had come on the scene.

"Sam." Wendy cocked her head at his daughter. "We've talked about this. *Always* is one of those words you need to use carefully. It's rare someone *always* does something."

"Sorry." Sam rolled her eyes and Wendy snorted.

The touch of humor helped Tom regain his footing. "What I was going to say was how nice it was seeing you smiling and happy for a change. I'm really proud of you for spending your time helping out here. And you said you liked to read, so this is perfect."

One of the parents stopped on their way out with their little boy. "Is this your dad?"

Sam nodded hesitantly.

The woman put her arm around Sam's shoulders. "She's really terrific." She squinted at Tom's name badge and added, "Dr. Farber. My husband's in ICU and I brought my son down here to give us both a nice break. You've done a wonderful job with Sam."

"Thank you," Tom said, glancing at his daughter. "She's a great kid."

His daughter's eyes widened, and her cheeks flushed and if he wasn't mistaken, he almost saw the hint of a smile before she hid it away. After the woman and her son left, Sam turned to Tom, her voice low. "Why are you being so nice? What's wrong?"

"Nothing's wrong." He crouched a little in front of her, praying he'd find the right thing to say. "Words can't express how sorry I am I've botched all of this up so badly. I let my disappointment with myself get the better of me and I'm deeply sorry."

Sam didn't respond. Just stood there, hugging her midsection, gaze narrowed on him.

"But if this is where you'd prefer to spend your time after school, I can stop worrying," he continued quietly.

His daughter dug the toe of her loafer into the shiny linoleum, pursing her lips. "I'd like that. Thank you."

"You're welcome," Tom said, straightening. He reached out and squeezed Sam's shoulder and, surprisingly, she let him. He wanted to pull her in for a hug, but a small crowd had formed once more at the center of the mat, waiting for the next story. Tom smiled at his daughter. "Looks like you're up again. Go get 'em, kiddo."

"Thanks, Dad." Sam returned his grin, before heading back to her chair to start another reading session. Tom and Wendy moved out into the hall. He still had a couple of hours left on his shift, but there was nothing pressing at the moment. "Want to grab a coffee in the cafeteria? My treat, to say thanks."

"Oh, um. Okay." Wendy walked back to her desk and told one of the other nurses where she was going then grabbed her phone. "Let's do it."

Doing his best to ignore the *double entendre* in her words, Tom pushed the Down button on the elevator, covertly checking out Wendy while they waited. Lavender scrubs, shiny hair pulled back into a ponytail again, pretty face natural, no makeup. Somehow, she managed to make even that outfit look sexy. His gaze skimmed over her narrow waist and full breasts, her pink lips, her dark eyes staring straight at him.

Busted.

She raised a brow and stepped on board the elevator.

Mind on the job, bub, as his dad always used to say.

They remained silent until they reached the cafeteria, where they each fixed their coffee then he paid the cashier. As they walked to a quiet table near the corner, it seemed Wendy could hold back her snark no longer.

"Do you like what you see?" she asked, giving him a coy look.

"Uh…" Tom's cheeks prickled with heat, despite the cool air-conditioning. He'd been caught red-handed. Then again, after the way he'd kissed her the other day, she had to know he liked her, so there was no sense denying it. He gave her a half smile. "Actually, I do."

His response seemed to shut her up quickly. He enjoyed teasing her more than he should.

Tom leaned back in his seat, keeping his walls intact the best he could because Wendy made it difficult. "Suffice it to say sometimes you make me forget my priorities."

"Being a parent does not sentence you to a life of celibacy, you know. Maybe getting laid once in a while might help take the edge off." She stopped short, fumbling her words slightly. He found her discombobulation adorable, just like the rest of her. "Not with me, of course. I didn't mean that. But with someone else. Go to dinner, watch a movie."

He rested his elbows on the table and leaned in closer, giving her a speculative look. "Why is it we never met *before* this whole thing with Sam? We're both from Anchorage."

"Probably because I rarely have time to leave the ER, except for my lunch breaks. And when I'm not working, I don't party, like some of the staff. I don't hang out at bars and I never take sexy doctors home with me."

His thoughts snagged on her last words and he blinked. "You think I'm sexy?"

She snorted again, and damn if he didn't feel that sound straight to his groin. "Based on our make-out sessions, I think it's safe to say I find you...*attractive*. Even if you can be a bit too persnickety at times."

"You didn't seem to find me too persnickety the other day when you were kissing me."

Wendy gave him a disparaging stare. "We should probably forget about that."

"I will if you will." Fresh heat prickled up from beneath the neckline of his scrubs, both because he really hadn't meant to bring that up again and also because now he was picturing Wendy naked in his bed.

Mind on the job, bub.

Wendy looked at her watch then shrugged, pretty pink color blossoming in her cheeks. "Discussion for another day, I'm afraid. My break's over soon. Did you invite me here for more than coffee or...?"

Actually, he'd been thinking about the conversation he'd overheard in the cafeteria, though he wasn't about to tell Wendy about his eavesdropping. So, instead, he tried to make it sound more like spontaneous inspiration. "I have an idea I need your help with. Please. We're friends now, after all. Aren't we?"

She gave him a funny look, then nodded slowly.

"Good. I don't think Sam's happy with her room."

"Maybe because it's four beige walls and a bed." Wendy sat back, her dark gaze narrowed. "She might have mentioned she was homesick."

"Perfect. I mean, not the fact that she's homesick. I don't want that at all. Just the opposite. What I want is for her to feel like her room is her space, to show her how important she is in my life. I was hoping you'd help me make that happen while she's away visiting my parents in Fairbanks over Memorial Day weekend. A surprise for when she returns."

Wendy seemed to consider that a moment, then said, "I think that's a great idea."

"Could you find out what colors Sam likes? What styles? Then you and I can discuss plans, maybe go shopping for stuff. If you're not busy, you could even come over during the long weekend and help me put it all together."

"Oh, I don't know about that part." Wendy sighed, her expression doubtful.

"C'mon. If you do come over, I'll treat you to lunch." His eyes met hers. "And a nice dinner. Five-star gourmet, if that's what you want." He wasn't above begging at this point. "Please?"

"I'll have to put in for the time off in the ER. No guarantees." She crossed her arms. "And it's going to take more planning than you think. There's a lot involved, to do things right."

"Know a lot about this stuff, do you?"

"Let's say I might have a small obsession with a certain reality TV renovation show." She frowned. "Aren't you working all weekend? I thought that's why you were sending Sam to your parents' place."

Busted again. He exhaled slowly and winced. "I am on call part of the weekend. But I also think Sam and I need some time apart. Please don't think less of me but it could do both of us some good. Give us a chance to catch our breath and maybe build on the small advances we've made over the past few weeks with your help. It's great being a father and having Sam with me, but I'm smart enough to know when I need a break."

"All parents need time off once in a while."

Relieved, he covered her hand with his, awareness zinging up his arm from their point of contact. Her skin was so soft, like silk beneath his fingertips. He couldn't help wondering if she felt that velvety all over.

Mind on the job, bub.

"Does that mean you'll help?" he asked.

She relaxed under his touch and sighed. "Like I said, I'll put in for the time and go from there. But I think it would make Sam super-happy so, yes. I'll help." He went to thank her, but she held up her free hand. "But this will take way more time than you think it will and three days isn't long for a room renovation. We should map out our plan of attack to make things easier. When's your next day off?"

"Tuesday," Tom said, a bit shocked she'd acquiesced so easily. "You can come to my apartment. I can order in dinner."

"No, we don't want Sam to overhear anything." She paused, as if coming to a decision. "You should probably come to my place instead."

Tom blinked, opened his mouth, then closed it again. Not only had she agreed to spend the weekend with him redecorating his daughter's room, she was inviting him over to her home as well. He wasn't sure exactly what all that signified, only that it was a big deal, for him at least. "Okay. Sounds like a plan."

"Perfect. Tuesday night it is. I'm off then too," she said, pulling free to take out her phone and type it into her calendar. "Say seven? I'll make dinner. Can the nanny stay with Sam?"

"Yep. I'll call her when I get back upstairs." He pushed to his feet. "Thank you."

She stood too, then looked at her watch again. "Got to get to work. I'll text you my address later."

With a nod and a wave Wendy took off back to the ER and Tom returned to L&D, feeling about a thousand pounds lighter and more hopeful than he had in years. For the first time in forever, things with Sam seemed to be on an upswing. And things with Wendy?

Well, he couldn't seem to wipe the stupid grin off his face or stop his heart from racing.

Tuesday couldn't get here soon enough.

CHAPTER NINE

INVITING TOM OVER to her apartment for dinner was turning out to have been a colossal mistake.

First, Wendy actually had to clean the place. Her decorating style was early thrift shop, circa 1994, with a definite hippie tone. She kept it *neat*, she just didn't keep it *clean*. She had spent most of the day dusting baseboards, pulling things off shelves and wiping under them, cleaning the corners of the bathroom and making sure everything appeared to have some semblance of order. Her cat, Dot, was no help at all, instead finding various sunny spots to curl up in.

Wendy opened the windows and aired the place out, turning on her essential oil mister to fill the air with eucalyptus and lavender. It made her feel more alert. Tom was the first guy she'd had to her apartment in a long time, and it was nearly seven now.

She'd bought groceries earlier, grateful she'd planned to cook a simple pasta dish with a marinara sauce, a rosemary focaccia and a tossed salad, with something chocolate from the bakery for dessert. All great first date food.

Even though, technically, this wasn't a date.

They were supposed to be meeting about Sam's room. And, yes, the kisses they'd shared had been off-the-charts good, but that was no reason to deviate from her life plans.

Now, if someone could just clue in her racing heart and tingling girlie parts, she'd be all set.

Everything was prepared. The salad was tossed and the bread sliced and cooling on the counter. She had the pasta and water and salt ready to boil once Tom arrived. Even the sauce was done, so she rearranged candles to keep busy, making sure the remote was next to the TV, and shooing Dot off the bed. She shouldn't be nervous, but this felt like more than just a dinner.

The idea both thrilled and terrified her.

Tom knew her secret and he was still here.

She wasn't naive enough to let herself believe that meant anything in the long term, but the more time she spent with him and Sam, the more she wanted to remain a part of their group. It had been so long since she'd felt a part of something other than her immediate family and she missed it more than she'd realized. Tom was the real deal and diving into a relationship with him would mean giving all of herself, one hundred percent involvement.

Only problem was, he was the whole package and she...*wasn't.*

Not with the Huntington's hanging over her head.

A few weeks earlier she'd have bailed on the whole idea, shut him down. But now things weren't so clear. She didn't want another meaningless one-night stand, but maybe, just maybe, this time was different.

Tom stood in the hallway outside Wendy's apartment and rang the bell, feeling like a nervous teenager. He kept reminding himself this wasn't a date, but that didn't seem to help. Plain truth was, he liked Wendy, way more than just a friend, and it was high time he admitted it. At least to himself. It wasn't like he needed to do anything about those feelings where she was concerned. In fact, it was best if he didn't, keeping them tucked deep inside where they belonged and didn't cause a mess.

Clean, tidy, ordered. That's how he liked things.

Wasn't it?

When Wendy had texted him her address, he hadn't realized he could walk here from his own place just two blocks down around the corner. They'd both picked Rogers Park to live in for whatever reason, probably the cheaper rents. He smiled, realizing she'd been so close all along.

The door opened, and he found his feet sniffed by a rotund cat. The feline was all black except for a large white patch atop its head and it seemed torn between rubbing up against him or running away and hiding. Tom lifted his eyes to meet Wendy's gaze and realized she wore the same expression as the cat. Maybe he wasn't the only one nervous about tonight.

The thought made his heart beat faster.

Breaking the awkward silence, she smiled and opened her door all the way, stepping back. "Please, come in."

He walked inside, holding a bottle of wine. Tom hadn't been sure, red or white, and had made a last-minute guess at the store, going for rosé to be safe. "Uh, I hope it goes with dinner."

She took it from him and her shoulders relaxed. "It's alcohol. It goes with everything."

"You do drink, right?" It occurred to him for the first time that maybe she didn't. His anxiety increased again. He should've called ahead, maybe brought dessert instead. Even flowers weren't safe nowadays. The one time he'd tried to go on a date since Sam had arrived, he'd brought a bouquet only to discover the poor woman had been allergic.

Good thing this wasn't a date, he reminded himself. No matter how much it felt like one.

"Are you kidding?" Wendy laughed. "Who in the medical profession *doesn't* drink?"

Tom chuckled, his tension dissipating under her easy charm. "Fair enough."

"Rosé is a lovely choice, thank you. Though

I have no idea whether it matches dinner." She walked into an open-style kitchen. On the counter, she'd prepared a meal. Salad, some sort of bread, pasta, dessert. Simple, to the point, no frills. Like Wendy.

Tonight she wore a pastel purple V-neck top and sleek black pants. No shoes. A little tattoo of a thunderbird near her second toe. She set the wine on the counter then rummaged through a nearby drawer and pulled out a corkscrew.

He walked over to the kitchen counter and she handed him the bottle, along with the opener. Light jazz music tinkled through the air from somewhere down the hallway. "Dinner doesn't have to be ready for a while," she said, turning off the burner under the sauce pot. The air smelled of lavender and garlic. "How about we enjoy a glass of wine—or three—and talk about the decorating."

"Sounds good." Tom took the corkscrew. "You live alone?"

"Yeah," she said, pulling two long-stemmed glasses from the cupboard. "This is only a one-bedroom and the owner lives on the third floor.

He likes having a nurse as a tenant. Been here for years. Just me and Dot."

"It's nice having another heartbeat around the house, isn't it?" he said, then felt stupid. Even after a year, the novelty of telling people about his kid hadn't worn off. And maybe he had turned into a gushing, geeky father. He wouldn't go back to his bachelor-pad life for a million years.

They took a seat on the sofa in her living room, at opposite ends, though he was still close enough to catch a hint of her perfume—warm and flowery with a hint of spice. It buzzed inside him like a firefly, making his nerve endings tingle.

Wendy tucked her bare feet beneath her and he noticed her tattoo again, along with her pink-painted toenails. Thoughts of kissing said toes until she moaned his name had him looking away fast. This whole not-a-date thing was going to be tougher to remember than Tom had imagined.

"So. Things between you and Sam seem to be thawing a bit." Wendy watched him over the rim of her glass as she relaxed back into the corner of the sofa. "That's good."

"Yeah, it is." Her soothing tone eased his stress and helped him open up. The wine he was guzzling didn't hurt either. Tom rested against the overstuffed cushions. "Thanks to you. I was at my wits' end there for a while."

"No!" Wendy gave a mock gasp and he chuckled.

"I tend to keep things bottled up inside. I'm a bit of a control freak sometimes, especially when I'm stressed."

"At last the truth comes out." Wendy winked, and something tightly coiled inside him unfurled. "How did you ever end up with Sam's mother?"

"There was something about Nikki. Maybe it was the whole opposites attracting thing but, whatever it was, I threw caution to the wind for once in my life and, well…you've seen how that turned out." He shrugged and downed the last of his wine. Before he knew it, Wendy was back with the bottle from the kitchen, topping up his glass and her own.

"Nikki worked as a barista at a coffee shop

around the corner from my medical school to pay the bills. We dated a few times, and by dated..." he gave Wendy a pointed look "...I mean we had sex. It was fun, letting loose and not caring. We were so happy at the beginning. She made me forget about all my responsibilities and cares. She had a talent for that. I did my best to make her happy.

"One night we got drunk and flew to Vegas and woke up married. Not exactly a match made in heaven. Afterward, we fought. A lot. I needed to focus on my studies. I set a schedule so I could fit everything in—our relationship, my career. But Nikki hated it. She hated rules and order of any kind. After a while, she hated me too.

"She walked out on me eighteen months after our wedding and filed for divorce. She was six months pregnant at the time. I continued to send her money when I could to help with the birth. I wanted to be there, but she refused. After Sam was born, she ended all communication. First call I received after more than a decade was from child welfare, informing me

Nikki had died of an accidental drug overdose and asking me to come and pick up Sam."

"God, I can't even imagine what that must've been like." She watched him closely.

Tom squeezed his eyes shut against the ache in his heart, reliving those awful memories of his return to Boston, the funeral, the dark days that had followed as he'd brought his child across the country to live with him, taking her away from the only home she'd ever known. "What I know for sure is that Nikki led Sam to believe I didn't want her. I've done my best to prove otherwise. Hopefully, someday my daughter will believe me."

"She will." Wendy reached over and clinked her glass against his. "We'll make sure of it."

"We will?" That came out more like a question than the definitive answer he'd wanted. Tom straightened, warmth from the wine and the beauty of Wendy's smile shimmering through him. "No. You're right. We will."

Tonight, this was exactly where he wanted to be, he realized. It had been so long, too long, since he'd felt comfortable, relaxed, unburdened with stress and worry. He and Sam were making progress together. Why, just this morning they'd had breakfast together, discussed their days. There hadn't been an eye roll or even a smirk in sight. Now he was with the woman who'd spiked his attraction for weeks. The woman who'd made it all possible. Yes, he needed her help with Sam, but he also enjoyed Wendy's company and sensed the friendship between them growing stronger. Maybe more.

More.

A month ago, he'd have denied wanting more. Even last week, he'd planned to decorate Sam's room, then walk away from Wendy and whatever this was brewing between them. He liked her. A lot. And, sure, he wanted her too. In truth, he'd been in a constant state of heightened arousal since they'd first met, but he had no idea how she felt about him. She seemed to like kissing him, but did she want more too?

After she'd shared the news of her mother's Huntington's disease with him, he knew he'd need to tread lightly around her. She was skittish, for good reason. Until she got those test results, her future was on hold. But perhaps that's the way she wanted it. Perhaps she was more terrified of knowing than she was willing to admit. Perhaps he could help her through that, like she'd helped him.

And perhaps he shouldn't worry about that tonight and concentrate on the now.

The alcohol fizzed through his system, releasing his inhibitions. He stared at the base of her throat as he sipped more wine, the fluttering pulse point there nearly making him groan.

His control slipped a little bit more.

Dinner was the focus here, he reminded himself. Food, wine, talking, putting together the perfect surprise for his daughter. He didn't do flings, he didn't do dangerous, wild, wicked. That had all ended with Nikki.

But fooling himself was getting harder and harder.

The truth was, Wendy made him want to be reckless.

She set her wine aside and bent to grab something off the coffee table, giving him a view right down her V-neck sweater. He nearly swallowed his tongue at the sight of her pretty lace bra.

Wendy grabbed an advertisement from the

newspaper and handed it to him. "I found the perfect comforter set and accessories for Sam's room. I went ahead and ordered them. They should be delivered before the weekend. Of course, if you hate them or they're too expensive I can cancel the order. Or I'll pay half. Or all if necessary. Honestly, I want her room to be amazing. The kind of room a girl would love to spend time in. A room she'd want to invite her friends over to see."

"Yes. That's what I want too, no matter the cost." Tom reviewed the results of what must've taken hours of research on the internet, grateful for the distraction.

"And I thought we could paint one wall this color." She held up a paint color swatch she'd gotten from the home improvement store and pointed to a shade marked with a red X. It reminded him of bubble gum. Not his thing but, then, he wasn't a preteen girl either. Whatever his daughter wanted was fine with him. "Sam told me you have hardwood floors, so this throw rug will offset the deep coloring of the wall perfectly." She pointed to a picture of a colorfully designed rug. "I couldn't find it in stock anywhere locally, so I had to order it too."

"Cool," he said. "What else?"

"Your daughter's favorite color is pink, for future reference. I say we paint the wall behind the bed solid pink then hang a few pictures and shelves to break it up. Like this." She pointed to the advert again. "She's going to love it."

Tom glanced down at the photos. "You've put a lot of time into this, huh?"

"No biggie. I told you, I like reality TV. Mainly the MedStar Network and the Home Channel's renovation shows. I picked up a lot of pointers there." She shrugged. "It's fun to have an outlet for all my pent-up creativity."

Tom could think of a few other pent-up things that it would be fun to release. With her.

He forced his attention back to the matter at hand.

"I like it. All of it." Tom studied the advertisement again. "Sam can do whatever she wants in her space. I want her to feel at home and welcome. I want her to be comfortable."

She considered him a moment. "You're a good dad."

"Really?" He shook his head. "Doesn't feel like it. Most of the time I feel like a failure."

"That's because you're way too hard on yourself. No one's perfect. Not even Tom Farber." Wendy met his gaze direct, her dark eyes sparkling with determination. "What do you want?"

You. He coughed and countered, "What do you mean?"

"Beneath all your rules and your perfectionist tendencies, what makes you happy?"

"Happy?" The word creaked out of his throat like an old floorboard, sounding as foreign as it felt. "I'm perfectly happy."

"Are you, really?"

When he didn't answer right away, too stunned by the words, Wendy must've taken it as a rejection. "Fine. Whatever. I've done what you asked me to do. You have pictures, store names and confirmation numbers on the orders I've placed. My work's done."

She started to get up, but he caught her arm.

"Wait," he said, unable to look away from her lips. "I know what I want."

Wendy stopped, her breath hitching.

He watched her watching him.

Hungry tension sizzled between them. Even the cat, sauntering past them, seemed to notice, and dashed in a new direction. Cars rumbled past outside, and field lights suddenly burst to life from the Little League game at Tikishla Park down the street. Their glow added a surreal shine to Wendy's eyes, fixed on him as he finished the rest of his wine in one long gulp.

He closed the space between them and slipped an arm around her waist, setting his empty glass aside then taking hers too, his touch gentle to avoid spooking her. He tightened his hold on her, his other hand splayed against her back between her shoulder blades. "I want you."

Her lips parted and, instead of pulling away, Wendy climbed onto his lap, straddling him. The friction set his entire body abuzz. With one finger, she traced a lazy path from his eyebrows, down the bridge of his nose. The rush he'd felt since the second they'd first met turned on a dime.

Tom kissed his way across her cheek to nibble on her earlobe. She felt so amazing against him. He sighed, raising his hand to cup her breast, her nipple pebbling under his touch.

Wendy stroked him through his clothing and he inhaled sharply. "I want you too."

"You do?" he asked, still not quite able to believe this was really happening.

"Oh, yeah. I do. Have for weeks."

At her admission, he gave in to his desire and kissed her deeply. She tasted of sweet wine and sinful promise. Delicious. "What about dinner?"

"Dinner can wait."

Tom laughed and stood, helping Wendy to her feet beside him. Yes, this was nuts. Yes, they'd only known each other a short time. Yes, it felt wild and dangerous and wicked, and Tom couldn't remember ever needing anything or anyone more in his life. He began tearing off his clothes, unbuttoning his blue oxford shirt, his normally precise and efficient fingers fumbling.

As he slid the shirt off his arms, Wendy joined him in disrobing, pulling her top off in one smooth motion, throwing it onto the sofa beside her. Her pants soon followed. The silken lilac bra and panties were so feminine and achingly delicate, he wanted to strip them off her with his teeth. Holding back, he drank in the vision of her instead while she did the same with him.

They both seemed to like what they saw.

He nodded. "Go ahead."

She frowned, hands on hips. "Go ahead what?"

"The bra."

"What about it?" she asked, looking down at herself.

"Take it off, please."

She frowned, as if considering his request, then darted down the hall. "Only if you catch me!"

Tom chased her, his legs constrained by too-tight pants.

Her bedroom was nicely decorated, homey, with large bedside tables and a multicolored silk scarf suspended from the ceiling, covering a light fixture. The last of the day's light poured in from the windows. Dusk would fall soon. He planned to be here as long as she'd have him.

Wendy's breath hitched as Tom caught her and undid the clasp on her bra.

Her gaze met his as it fell to the floor.

CHAPTER TEN

WENDY FELT OVERWHELMED, trying to play off how much Tom affected her.

Like this happened *every* Tuesday.

Blues music floated through the air, the smoky tones of saxophone adding to the perfection in the room. He stripped down to his boxer briefs, the fluid lines of his powerful thighs making her yearn. She could have watched him all day.

He had other ideas.

Tom pulled her onto the patchwork quilt covering her bed. The comfortable mattress invited them to stay awhile. The hot press of his chest against hers made her shiver with arousal, gooseflesh prickling on her exposed arms and breasts, her nipples tightening.

His slow, seeking kisses made her arch against him with barely restrained urgency. He shifted his hips and his hard length pressed into the heat between her legs, the frustration of the two thin swaths of cloth separating them making her gasp.

The song ended, and an Etta James tune came on. He smiled, propping his head on his hand and looking at her with delight, taking his sweet time. She reveled in his attention, doing some looking herself.

He was exquisite, and she ran her hands over his toned, tanned chest, down to his flat abs then to his hips. His sharp inhalation told her what he wanted. She reached for his length and he watched her, then gripped her wrist, forcing her to pause.

"No rush." Tom released her, sliding his palm along her side. The slow journey up the curve of her waist to the edge of her breast, then to her shoulder, was sweet torture.

"You're so beautiful," he whispered, rolling her onto her back, taking her nipple into his mouth, the ache inside her becoming nearly unbearable. His calves brushed against hers, his lips feathering a line across the valley of her breasts to give equal attention to both taut peaks.

A hum of tension built slowly inside her as his kisses moved southward. He took his time lowering her panties, then caressed his way back up her legs before returning to lie beside her.

"Fair is fair." She slipped her hands under the waistband of his boxer briefs, sliding them down to his feet with a deftness that defied her earlier nerves.

Both fully nude, they paused. Their mutual appreciation made her laugh.

"Something funny?" he asked as he looked down at their naked bodies.

It would have been so easy to resort to her usual sarcastic wisecracks, but she took the more difficult, honest route. "I don't know why I'm laughing. It's just..."

"Joy," he said, brushing a lock of hair from her cheek as she lay back down.

"Joy?"

"Yeah. I feel it too." He moved lower to rest on his stomach between her thighs, kissing his way down her abdomen, his tongue tracing slow circles around her belly button, making her muscles quiver.

"You do?" Then she gasped as his tongue traced lightly over her damp folds. Her fingers tangled in his hair and she fought against a riptide of desire.

"God, yes." His warm mouth moved on her and she closed her eyes, lifting her hips. With his gentle ministrations he brought her to the brink of ecstasy then eased her over the edge. She clutched his shoulders, panting, bucking as waves of orgasm crashed over her.

Tom kissed his way back up her body and she reached down to stroke his length, finding him hard and ready. He was right. Joy was exactly what she felt.

The music changed once more to a slow melodic piano and string ensemble as she wrapped her hand around his erection, fingers struggling to touch. He stopped her, moving over her, giving her access to all of him.

"I want to be inside you, Wendy," Tom said, asking permission, his voice husky.

"And I want you inside me." She grabbed a condom from the nightstand drawer then handed it to him. He tore it open before smoothing it on.

Wendy batted her lashes, unable to remember a time when she'd had more fun during sex. Usually, it was a frantic, sweaty race to the finish line. But Tom made her chest ache with sweetness, his smile making her fall a little more. He was the kind of guy she could spend more time with, get to know better and better, love… A niggle of warning echoed inside her head, but she shoved it aside. There'd be plenty of time for doubts later. Right now, she wanted him, fiercely.

"You're so amazing." He rolled onto his back and pulled Wendy atop him.

Enjoying the power, she touched his chest, his neck, his face, tracing his lips with her fingers as if trying to memorize him. She ached to have him. His hands roamed her belly, her rib cage, cupped her breasts again.

Then he pushed inside her, the pleasure making her forget everything else. Their gazes met, and she leaned forward for another kiss, their bodies moving in rhythm, her need growing with each thrust as her second climax loomed.

"Wendy," he whispered. "Are you…?"

"Close?" She groaned. "Oh, yeah."

Tom gripped her hips, setting the pace. A few strokes was all it took to send her toppling over the brink once more. Then Tom rolled her beneath him and drove into her hard and fast until his body tightened with orgasm too. As the intense sensations receded, he relaxed beside her, their breaths ragged. A loud *crack* pierced the air, followed by the cheers of the crowd at the baseball field.

"A home run," Wendy said as Tom lay beside her. She cradled his cheek, his bright blue eyes meeting hers with a depth of kindness that would have terrified her even a week prior.

"I'd certainly give you a standing ovation," he said, waggling his brows.

"You just did," she said, laughing.

He got up to use the bathroom then returned to gather her close, spooning her. The man's body was one big heating pad, and she wondered what it would feel like in the dead of winter, cozy in bed with Tom, no longer needing the cat to warm her feet.

Then her stomach growled.

"We forgot to eat," he said.

The room had darkened, and she snapped

on the bedside light. They both searched the floor for their clothes. By the time Tom pulled on his pants and shirt, she was down the hall. His footsteps echoed behind her as she opened the refrigerator door then grabbed a few items from the cupboard. By the time he reached the kitchen, she was in front of the stove, turning the burner up under the pot of water.

"More wine?" she asked, her hands trembling as she held the bottle, her nerves returning as awkwardness set in again. "How do we act around each other after *that*?"

Tom drank down half his glass of wine in one big gulp. He reached for her and they looked at each other for a minute, neither breaking eye contact, relaxing layer by layer. "It's all new territory for me too. With Sam in my life."

"This is hard," Wendy said, forcing the words out past the tension constricting her throat. "With my past and the HD, I don't have relationships. I have flings. Casual stuff." He opened his mouth, but she held up one hand. "I don't *do* emotional openness. I do sex, I do fun, I do sarcasm…"

"Then maybe it's time you tried something new." He pulled her closer.

She stepped out of the embrace, turning away. Her hands shook as she stirred the water, pouring the pasta in bit by bit. She'd been shaken by what they'd experienced together. It had been sweet and sexy and so far past her usual quickie encounters she didn't know how to handle it.

When he spoke again, Tom's tone was soft and soothing, as if she were a nervous colt, ready to bolt at the slightest provocation. Her heart was certainly racing like a thoroughbred's. "I don't want more from you than you want to give."

She closed her eyes and took a deep breath. "When did this get complicated?"

"Relationships are always complicated."

"Please don't say that."

He tilted his head. "What? That this is a relationship? What should I call it, then?"

"I don't know."

His stomach growled loudly.

"The perfect response," she said, resuming her cooking, glad of a distraction. "Let's just take things a day at a time, okay? I'm a lousy cook, by the way."

"I doubt you're lousy at anything."

"Oh, trust me, once you get to know me you'll learn I'm lousy at lots of things." A few minutes later, she pulled the pasta pot off the stove and drained the boiling water, clouds of steam hot against her face.

"What can I do to help?"

Wendy shoved her feelings down deep, as she always did, and forced a grin she didn't feel as she poured the pasta into a large serving bowl then stirred in the sauce. "Could you put the salad on the table, please? And the bread?"

He did as she asked. They sat down. Dinner was quiet.

"This is good," he said at last.

"You're just being polite."

"I don't say anything I don't mean. It's good. Thank you."

She gave him an incredulous stare. "We just had sex, Tom, you don't need to butter me up."

"Hey, at my place, this would be a luxurious meal."

"Sam told me you guys eat a lot of takeout."

Wendy smiled. "What would you serve if you invited me over for dinner?"

He shrugged. "Pizza or Thai, probably. Sam's been on an Asian kick lately."

"Don't you ever cook?" She reached for more salad, surprised when he took her hand.

"No time," he said. "Hey, relax, okay? We'll get through this and go slow."

"I'm sorry, I have no framework for how to behave with someone like you."

"Like me?"

"Yeah. Nice. Normal. Like I said, I don't spend a lot of time with the guys I...well, you know. This is the first time I've had a man over for dinner in a long time."

Headlights flashed on the wall and car engines roared to life as the game ended across the street and people made their way back to their lives, the fun diversion over.

Fun and diversion had been her shell. Without it, Wendy wasn't sure how she'd cope.

"After this, do you want to watch some TV with me?" she asked, pushing her food around on her plate with her fork, hoping to get this train back on the tracks. "*Renovation Station* is on tonight. Maybe we can get some more tips for Sam's room? Do you watch that show?"

Tom shrugged. "No. I don't watch much of anything. I work hundred-hour weeks."

Sighing, she refilled their wineglasses and they finished their meal in silence. Afterward, once they'd cleared the table and put away the leftovers, she took his hand and walked him toward the living room. "Tonight *Renovation Station*. Next time we'll do the MedStar Network."

"Will there be a next time?" he asked, settling on the sofa then wrapping his arm around her shoulders as she snuggled in beside him.

Wendy relaxed, telling herself she could do this, take it one step at a time, one day at a time, and keep her heart and her life intact. She chinked her glass against his, a lump of anxiety clogging her throat even as she winked at him. "If you play your cards right."

CHAPTER ELEVEN

WENDY AWOKE THE next morning to a heavy, muscled thigh trapping her to the bed. Her ears buzzed, and her head felt fuzzy. It took her a moment to realize the ringing was coming from her phone. She blinked her eyes open to find Tom, naked, half on top of her, snoring.

Memories of the previous night flooded back. He'd carried her to bed after watching a marathon of reality TV and finishing the wine. They'd had sex again. It had been incredible. It had been everything she'd hoped for and more. It had been hot and slow and sweet, as if they had all the time in the world and…

OhGodohGodohGod.

Her eyes opened wide as she came fully awake. The phone. It was Wednesday. She was scheduled to work. What if they needed her earlier? What if something had happened with Sam? Tom had mentioned last night that he'd booked the nanny to stay with her all night, but what if she needed him this morning?

Sitting up fast and fumbling for her phone on the nightstand with clumsy fingers, Wendy nearly dropped it twice before finally answering. "Hello?"

"Hey!"

Aiyana.

Wendy swallowed hard to dislodge her heart from her throat and squinted into the too-bright room, searching for her alarm clock. Almost eight thirty. Ugh. She struggled to form a coherent sentence without having had her daily caffeine infusion yet. "What's going on?"

Tom stirred beside her, yawning and stretching before sitting up too, giving her enough eye candy to last a lifetime. "Who is it?" he mumbled. "What's happening? Is Sam all right? Is there an emergency at the hospital?"

"Who's that?" Aiyana whispered over the phone line. "Where are you?"

"I'm home," Wendy said. Less was definitely more in this situation. She was still trying to wrap her head around the fact she'd slept with Tom Farber. She certainly wasn't ready to share that news with anyone else yet. Besides, talking wasn't her strong suit in the morning, especially with a gorgeous man at her side. A gorgeous, naked man who was now nuzzling the nape of her neck all the way up to her ear where she held the phone.

She shivered and glanced back at him over her shoulder. In the daylight, he was even hotter, all big and rumpled and protective and…

"That was a man's voice," Aiyana said, her tone suspicious. "Are you with the OB doc?"

"She is," Tom said near the phone before she could stop him. He chuckled, the sound rumbling through her and disrupting all her good intentions.

"Oh, my God!" Aiyana exclaimed, so loudly Wendy had to hold the phone away from her ear. "Naughty girl. Good for you."

Wendy squeezed her eyes shut, cringing. "Please don't make a big deal about this."

Tom kissed her cheek then got up and padded to the bathroom. She admired the view, missing his warmth already, then gathered the covers closer around her like a shield.

"This is fantastic! I knew there was something sparking between the two of you that day in my hospital room." Aiyana's happiness and excitement radiated through her words. "How long have you two been together?"

Wendy sighed and rubbed her eyes. "We're not really together."

"What are you, then?" Her sister-in-law sounded confused.

"Making it up as we go along."

"But you let him spend the night. You *never* let guys spend the night."

"Look, it just happened, okay? We didn't plan it. In fact, we've sort of been trying to avoid it. Then I agreed to help him with a project for his daughter and he came over last night to make shopping lists and we had some wine and one thing led to another." She groaned and covered her face. Last night had been a whole lot more than that, at least for her, but Wendy wasn't willing to share that yet. She tried to make it all sound as casual as she could to throw Aiyana off the scent. "We fell asleep halfway through a marathon of *Renovation Station*. It's no big deal."

"It's a huge deal." Damn. Her sister-in-law

wasn't convinced at all. "Now you really have to get your test results."

"What? No, I don't. Why?" The bathroom door opened and the sounds of Tom's footsteps echoed as he walked out of the bedroom and down the hall toward the kitchen, still totally naked and apparently totally unashamed. It all felt so comfortable and right and normal that her stomach knotted. She couldn't let herself get used to this. Nope. "There's no reason to go there, Aiyana. I'm careful. I always use protection. Double protection. Condoms and the Pill. We had one night together. It's not like we're married or anything."

The warm aroma of freshly brewed coffee soon filled the air. The sounds of Tom fumbling around in her kitchen jangled her nerves. He'd made her coffee. Of all the nice things he'd done for her, that went right to the top of Wendy's list. Had to love a man who made you coffee. Her heart skipped. Or not. Love wasn't part of this equation. Annoyed with herself and her unwanted, seemingly unstoppable growing feelings for Tom, Wendy growled. "Why are you calling?"

"To complain about my boring life. But yours is much more interesting!" Aiyana laughed at Wendy's annoyed snarl then lowered her voice. "Okay, give me the scoop. Is he good in bed?"

"I'm hanging up now." Wendy scooted up to rest against the headboard, clutching the covers to her chest as Tom walked back in, carrying two mugs of coffee. He handed one to her and kissed her softly. Yep. He was good in bed. Good out of bed too. Hell, Tom was good pretty much everywhere. No man had ever brought her coffee in bed. Then again, no man had ever had the chance to either. "I'll call you later. Bye."

She ignored Aiyana's protests and clicked off her phone then tossed it aside.

"I need a shower," Tom said as she took a much-needed sip of caffeine. "Want to join me?"

Wendy really wanted to—man, did she. But if they got in the shower together, there was a good chance they'd not come out for a long time. Besides, more sexy times with Tom right now wouldn't help her get her thoughts in order. "Uh, my shift starts at ten. Maybe next time?"

"Definitely next time." He kissed her again then went back into the bathroom alone. She sat there, listening to the sound of running water and imagining what next time would be like. Could she survive a "next time"? Did she even want to try? Her chest ached at the realization that, yes, she did. And damn if that didn't scare her most of all.

Tom exited a few minutes later, wet, with a towel around his hips. Wendy dodged his attempt to pull her into his embrace and raced to the bathroom without saying a word, shutting the door then having a quick wash and shampoo herself before rinsing off. By the time she came out, Tom was fully dressed in his clothes from the night before, the color of his shirt making his eyes look an even deeper blue. He smiled and picked up both their empty mugs, heading back to the kitchen, while she dressed in a fresh set of lavender scrubs, the beep of the microwave her soundtrack. She towel-dried her hair before joining him in the kitchen.

"Are you on call today?" she asked.

"No. I need to catch up on sleep. My shift starts tonight. Twenty-four hours. I juggled my schedule and picked up some extra work this week so I can be off for Memorial Day."

"Right." The three days of togetherness loomed ahead of her—so promising, so precious, so potentially dangerous to her heart and the well-built barriers surrounding it. Her defenses were already starting to crack and if she let them down completely, she wasn't sure how she'd cope.

Now you really have to get your test results.

Aiyana's words drifted through her mind again, making her temples throb.

Or maybe that was all the wine they'd had the night before. Hard to tell.

Either way, Wendy avoided Tom's gaze, feeling fragile and way too vulnerable for her comfort. "Speaking of Memorial Day weekend, I managed to cash in some of my vacation time and pull some strings too, so I'm off all three days. If you want, I can pick up the stuff from the department store on Friday night after work and bring it over to your place after your parents pick up Sam. That way we can avoid spoiling the surprise."

"Sounds good." He stepped forward and

slipped his arm around her waist to pull her closer, but she dodged away.

If she wanted to be on time for work, she needed to leave soon, but Tom was still standing there, looking far too tempting. Finally, he put his empty mug in the sink and held out his hand. "You need to go. Walk me to the door."

She did. They stood on her threshold. Out of nowhere Dot appeared to nuzzle Tom's legs.

He looked down, frowning. "Ah, the elusive feline. I think he likes me. Or is it a she?"

"Dot's a girl," Wendy said.

This time when he put his arm around her waist, she didn't stop him. He pulled her closer and she couldn't resist burying her face against his neck, burrowing into his arms. He smelled of soap and a trace of his citrus cologne left over from last night. Wendy couldn't get enough, might never get enough of him. Finally, after one long last kiss, she nudged him on his way, needing the last few minutes to get ready and clear her head.

Sighing, Wendy headed back to her bedroom, resisting the urge to run to the window to watch Tom walk away. A quick blow-dry and another giant mug of coffee later she was finally ready to head to Anchorage Mercy.

The day went quickly at least. Before she knew it, it was three o'clock and time for her lunch break. Wendy grabbed her wallet and headed down to the cafeteria to meet Sam.

"Hey," Wendy said, placing her tray down opposite Sam and pulling out a chair. She did her best to act cool and not let on at all that things had changed between her and Tom. After all, they'd technically not discussed exactly *what* was happening between them. For all Wendy knew, it was just another fling. That's how she was going to look at it anyway, no matter what her stupid heart said. To dream of anything more was ridiculous, especially with her situation. She poured dressing on her salad and forced a smile she didn't quite feel. "How's it going? You ready for your trip next weekend?"

Sam eyed her speculatively. "Yup. What's going on with you and my dad?"

For a moment, it felt like the earth shifted beneath Wendy's feet. Heat prickled her cheeks as she fiddled with her silverware. *Play it cool. Play it cool.*

"Nothing. Why?"

"Do you like him?" Sam picked up an apple and bit into it, her expression quizzical. "I mean, *like* him like him?"

"Your dad's very nice. Why are you asking me this?"

"No reason." Sam watched her closely for a beat or two more before shrugging and looking away. "He and I have been talking more, getting along better, I guess. He just seems to, I don't know, get all glowy when he talks about you."

"Glowy?" The word stuck in Wendy's constricted throat and came out as more of a squeak. A strange warmth spread outward from her core to her extremities at the thought that Tom might be smitten with her before she tamped it down.

This was a "no smitten" zone.

Regardless of how amazing it felt.

Time to change the subject. "I hope that means you're feeling better about your visit to Fairbanks this weekend. Tell me more about what your grandparents have planned."

"They called the other night and Dad put them on speakerphone." Wendy suppressed a smile at her easy use of the endearment now. Progress indeed. Good for Tom. Good for Sam too.

"Grandpa Albert has a boat, so we'll probably go out on the water," Sam said, around another bite of apple. "I have to wear a life jacket, in case I fall in, but he's going to teach me to swim while I'm there too. They have a pool." She took a sip of milk. "And Grandma's going to take me to the craft store to get supplies, so she can teach me how to knit. I've wanted to learn since I was back in Boston. There's a couple of girls at school who do crafts and we can work on stuff together."

"That's awesome." Wendy kept her tone casual, so glad Sam sounded excited about a trip she'd been dreading just a week or so ago. And the fact she seemed to be making friends here? That was maybe the best part of all, considering how alone and isolated Sam had felt. Opening up the lines of communication between Tom and his daughter had helped them both progress by leaps and bounds, and Wendy felt honored to have played a tiny part. She grinned, genuinely this time. "Sounds fun and you'll have plenty to keep you busy."

"Yeah. Grandpa said I should be able to swim by myself by the end of the weekend."

Wendy gave her a thumbs-up, since her mouth was full of salad.

"Do you know how to swim?"

"I grew up with three older brothers. What do you think?" Wendy shrugged. "But I didn't have someone teach me. When I was eight, my dad and brothers took me out in Cook Inlet and dropped me in. That's how I learned. Be grateful."

"Ugh. That sounds awful." Sam made a face. "I'm sorry."

"It's fine." Wendy chuckled. "I'm a survivor."

"Me too," Sam said, turning serious. "Hey, since you and my dad are friends now, will you do something for me?"

Wendy stopped in midsip of her vitamin water, her tension ratcheting up again. "If I can."

"I'm worried about my dad."

"Oh?" He'd seemed fine when he'd left her apartment that morning. "Why?"

"Will you keep an eye on him while I'm gone? I'm going to call him every day. But I'd like someone close to make sure he's okay."

"Sam." Wendy reached across the table to take the girl's hand, sensing there was more to this than just normal concern. "Your dad will be fine. Don't worry. Nothing will happen."

"He's all I have now," she said, a slight catch in her voice. "What if I'm gone and he…?"

Wendy's chest squeezed with emotion. She'd felt the same way for months after her mom had died, not letting her dad or her brothers out of her sight and worrying herself sick anytime she had to leave home, thinking they'd die and leave her just like her mother had.

But this was an assurance she could easily give to Sam, since she and Tom would be spending the weekend together, even if Wendy had to fudge the truth a bit. "I promise I'll check in on your dad while you're gone."

"Thanks." Sam slid a piece of paper across the table to her. "I wrote down his cell number, so you could call him. If you want. And our address."

Wendy grinned. She already had both, but Sam didn't know it. "I'm glad we're friends."

Sam smiled back. "Me too."

"Now, go on your trip and have fun."

"I will." Sam squeezed Wendy's hand tight. "I'll miss our chats while I'm gone."

"Me too," Wendy said, squeezing back.

By ten o'clock on Friday night, Tom and Wendy finally stood outside his apartment.

"Having the paint delivered was a good call," he told Wendy, looking at where the superintendent of his building had neatly arranged the cans to the side of his entryway.

He unlocked the door and gestured her inside then followed, kicking the door shut behind them with the edge of his foot before putting down the bags of stuff he'd carried for what had seemed like miles through the gigantic warehouse home improvement store.

She carefully unloaded their purchases, pushing her hair away from her face. "I can't believe we got all this done in one night."

They'd accomplished more shopping in four hours than Tom typically did in a month. Heck, three months. Normally, he'd feel exhausted after all that, but instead he felt energized. Wendy's enthusiasm was contagious, her determination to find the perfect things and her excitement when she did had made every minute of their expedition fun.

He and Sam were lucky to have her on their side.

Their side.

After a year, he'd gotten to the point where he'd begun thinking of Sam and himself as a "we," a unit, a family. Was he ready to add another person to that mix? Should he even consider it at this point? The last thing Sam needed in her life was more upheaval and he certainly never wanted to be the cause of it. Especially with Wendy's test results still unknown. Still, he was finding it harder and harder to not think of the three of them as a cohesive group.

Those warning sirens wailed in his head again before he squelched them.

Mind the job, bub.

Enjoy the weekend. Decorate Sam's room. Keep things light and fun and easy.

As he repeated that mantra over and over in his head, Tom fiddled with the packages of tape and nails and brushes Wendy had placed atop the island, arranging them into neat stacks.

An old niggle of doubt bored through him before he stopped it.

This was fine. This wasn't the same as before in Boston. Wendy certainly wasn't Nikki, and this certainly wasn't a prelude to marriage. They were just two consenting adults having a good time together and getting a project done. Beyond that, who knew? He forced himself to stop messing with the packages and jammed his hands into his pockets. Tonight he planned to find out exactly where Wendy stood on things, make sure they were on the same page. As a loner bachelor, he wouldn't have cared. But now, as a father, he owed it to Sam to be responsible.

He'd promised Wendy they'd take things slowly, and they would.

But the control-loving part of him wouldn't

rest until he at least knew the direction they were headed.

Wendy covered her mouth and yawned, squinting at him. "Sorry. I was up at six."

"Coffee?" he asked.

"Always." She walked down the hall to peek into Sam's room. "We can prep for painting tonight and get started first thing tomorrow."

"Or we could relax tonight and hit it hard in the morning." After his parents had picked up Sam that afternoon, he'd spent part of his time boxing up his daughter's things to make sure they didn't get damaged during the renovation. They were ready to go for tomorrow. Tonight he had more important things on his mind. "Can I talk to you about something?"

"Sure." She took a seat on a stool at the breakfast bar and rested her chin in her hand, her expression thoughtful as she watched him make the coffee then push Start. "What's going on?"

"Sam and I discussed a few things earlier, before my parents picked her up." He took a deep breath, finding it harder than he'd expected to broach the subject, especially knowing how

Wendy usually balked at any mention of long-term relationships or commitment.

"Sam's been thinking a lot about what happened to her mother, unpacking a bunch of emotions around that. Which is great, healthy. I'm afraid, though, it also got her thinking about what will happen to her if I..." He raked a hand through his hair, knowing what a volatile subject it was with Wendy's potential Huntington's disease towering over them. In the end, he forced the words out in a fast tumble. "Well, she wondered what will happen to her if I die too. I told her that wasn't likely to happen for a long time. I'm healthy as a horse, according to my last physical, but when she gets an idea in her head she won't quit. Gets that from her mother."

Wendy raised a brow.

"Okay, fine. She gets that from me too." The coffee maker gurgled away, and he pulled out the carafe to pour them each a mug then put it back into place to continue to fill. Tom passed Wendy the cream before putting a splash in his own, his gaze locked on her puckered lips as she blew on her steaming mug. He could think of all sorts of fun things she could use that mouth of hers for. He coughed and turned away fast to distract himself.

"Anyway, I told her she'd go to live with my parents in that event. But it also got me thinking about us. About you." He leaned back against the counter. "About your test results."

She winced slightly, then tilted her head, not looking at him. "I'm prepared."

Tom narrowed his eyes. "Prepared for what? Prepared to find out your results?"

"Why are you bringing this up all of a sudden?" Wendy frowned, her voice edged. "When I first told you, you acted like it wasn't a big deal. Now all of a sudden it is? Fine. I've taken precautions either way. I have a will. I made sure to lease an apartment on the ground level of my building, in case I might need wheelchair access one day. Anything else you'd like to give me the third degree on?"

"I didn't mean to upset you, Wendy." Tom hung his head. "And I'm sorry if you felt like this came out of the blue. It's just taken me a while to process my thoughts on everything. And now that we're sleeping together, and things have gotten more serious between us, I need to consider how all this will affect Sam too. I'm just trying to do the right thing, the responsible thing, for everyone involved."

Her expression hardened. "I see. I've been nothing but honest with you since the start of all this. I told you about my family history of Huntington's disease. I don't tell many people about that, Tom. If and when I decide to find out my results, it will be my choice and on my timetable. I like Sam and I like you. Way more than I should, but long-term relationships aren't something I ever considered for myself. I'm doing the best I can here, Tom. What more do you want from me?"

Everything.

Given her current reactions, though, Tom knew better than to say it. His heart ached knowing what a burden she must carry because of her mother's disease, but he also wanted to tell her he'd be there for her no matter what, if she'd let him. "I've done some research into HD and they've made great strides managing the disease recently. Still no cure, but lots of clinical trials for new drugs for treatment, plus support networks and—"

"And did your research also tell you that only ten percent of people at risk for the disease choose to have the predictive testing done? It's a numbers game on both sides. There's a fifty-fifty chance I have it. My three siblings tested negative, so…" She scowled down at the counter. "You know, let's not talk about this right now. This weekend is supposed to be fun, not serious."

Tom stood on the opposite side of the breakfast bar from her and frowned, not quite ready to leave the deeper waters. "Okay. But eventually we'll need to talk about it. I won't push you, but you deserve peace of mind, Wendy. You deserve to be happy too."

She gave him a startled glance. Yep, he'd smacked right into the brick wall of her fears.

He came around to sit on the stool beside hers and took her hands.

Wendy tensed beneath his touch, pulling away, a haunted look in her dark eyes. "You say you'll be there for me if things don't go well, but you have no idea what it's like. My mother's death was awful and horrible and terrifying. I'd never want to put you or Sam through that. Can't we just enjoy our time together, for as long as it lasts?"

They were both dressed casually tonight in jeans. He had on a black T-shirt and she wore a pretty pink top that hugged her curves to perfection. While he wasn't giving up on the subject, having her so close persuaded him to put it off, at least a little longer.

It had been days since that torrid night at her apartment and he'd not been able to stop thinking about a repeat performance. Wendy looked so damned sexy with her long legs and sleek hair and infinitely kissable lips. He ached from wanting her.

Putting a foot on either side of her stool, Tom effectively caged her between his thighs. They looked at each other as the air around them thickened with lust. Her gaze dropped to his rapidly hardening groin before flickering back to his eyes.

"One day at a time, huh?" he said. "What about the nights?"

"What about them?" Desire made her voice husky.

He placed his hands on her knees, his thumbs rubbing gentle circles on the soft denim. "Here we are."

Tom held his breath, stayed quiet, waited. The next move was hers.

Wendy leaned closer still to rest her hands on his chest. "Promise me one thing." She slowly traced her fingers down his torso to his waistband, then cupped his straining length through his jeans. He needed her so badly, he nearly embarrassed himself on the spot.

"Anything." At this moment Tom would've given her the universe to have her keep touching him. "Anything at all."

"After this weekend." Her hand kept moving over his erection. Up and down. Tip to base. Over and over. Lulling him into a passion-filled stupor. "Once Sam comes home and we get back to our regular lives, no matter what happens between us, promise me things won't get weird."

The motion of her hand made it difficult for him to focus, but he did his best, knowing there was more on the line here than just sex. Over the past few weeks he'd come to value Wendy's friendship as much as their sizzling sexual chemistry. Even if he never broke through her barriers and got past her fears, even if this weekend was all they ever had, he'd do everything in his power to ensure it didn't interfere with them in the future. "I promise."

"Good." Wendy drew back to pull off her top, revealing a black lace bra this time. He'd thought the purple one from the other night was sexy, but this one was off-the-charts hot. She tossed her shirt aside then smiled. "Get those clothes off, mister."

Gladly. Tom didn't think he'd ever disrobed so fast in his life.

Once he was naked, she guided him down to the hardwood floor between the breakfast bar and the island, then straddled his hips.

"What about you?" He palmed her denim-covered butt and guided her right where he wanted her, unable to stop grinding against her, needing more.

"You in a hurry, Dr. Farber?"

He didn't want to be, but he was primed and ready. Oh. So. Ready.

"We'll go slow next time, Nurse Smith." He reached up to unclasp her bra then slid it off. Tom pulled her in for a kiss, savoring the feel of her bare breasts against his chest, her nipples hard and straining. God, he'd craved her for days, since the last time they'd been together, yearning to feel the curve of her waist, the smoothness of her skin, her soft hair, her lips.

Time passed in a series of deep, passion-filled kisses and desperate caresses. He felt cocooned in a place he never wanted to leave. The temperature seemed to rise in the room. Their moans grew louder, their movements more urgent.

Then Wendy pulled away and shimmied out of her jeans and panties all at once. He pointed to his crumpled jeans on the floor and she pulled out a condom from the back pocket. He nearly climaxed when she put it on him, stopping to place a single, delicate kiss atop his erection before positioning herself over him again. Slowly Wendy sank down and Tom entered paradise.

He thrust into her while she rode him, burying himself as deep inside her as possible, taking a moment to savor the tight, wet heat surrounding him.

"More." She dug her fingers into his shoulders and he gave her what she wanted, what he wanted, driving into her. She cried out as he leaned up on his elbows to take one of her nipples into his mouth.

"So good." She moaned and rocked against him, her rhythm steady and fast.

He met her thrust for frantic thrust. His scrotum tightened. Her body stiffened.

"Don't stop," Wendy said, pulling him in for another kiss.

"Never," Tom whispered against her lips as wave after wave of pleasure crashed over them.

Several hot, sweaty, fantastic minutes later, she pulled back, still panting. "I've never done it on the kitchen floor before."

He nuzzled up close to her ear. "Glad I could be your first."

"Yeah?" Wendy grinned. "Trust me, you're my first in a lot of ways."

Tom's heart leaped at those words, but he tamped it down. It was sex talk, that was all. To read anything more into it was asking for trouble. He grinned and focused only on this moment, this woman, this night. "Let's move to my bed and I'll see if I can add more firsts to the list."

CHAPTER TWELVE

WENDY AWOKE EARLY the next morning and found the bed beside her empty, except for a note from Tom that he'd gone out for his morning jog and would see her soon. Just as well, she supposed, since she really needed a bit of time herself to regroup after last night.

Being with Tom again had been good. Maybe too good.

Ugh. She flopped back into her pillow and covered her eyes with her arm. Bad enough she'd let things get this far. Normally, she would've been long gone after the first night they'd spent together in her apartment, spurned his continued advances and gotten on with her lonely, boring life. Except she couldn't now, and not just because she'd agreed to help him with Sam either.

Of course, that commitment was a big part of it. She loved the kid too, no two way's about it. They had so much in common and she saw so much of herself in young Sam that it was like looking in a mirror sometimes. But that love came at a price, namely that she was losing her battered heart to Tom and it scared the hell out of her.

Resigned, she got up and padded to the bathroom to get ready. After a shower and tugging on clothes, she automatically reached into her makeup kit and pulled out her birth-control pill pack. Punched out the day's pill, then froze. Blinked and counted then blinked again.

Recounted.

Damn. She'd missed one. In twelve years, that had never, ever happened.

She took a deep breath. Exhaled. Inhaled again.

Okay, fine. No big deal. People messed up their birth control all the time. One pill shouldn't be the end of the world. These past few weeks had been more hectic than usual and having Tom in her life had disrupted her normal routine and she'd forgotten one stinking pill. She counted back to find it had been that Tuesday when he'd come over to her apartment to talk about the decorating plans. The first time they'd spent the night together…

Damn. Damn. Damn.

Pulse racing and hands shaking, Wendy swallowed down that day's dose then shoved the pink plastic pack back into her overnight bag before heading out to the kitchen in a fog.

They'd used condoms too, so the chances of pregnancy were extremely small.

But how could she have been so stupid? She never forgot her pills.

Because her feelings for Tom were a distraction.

A hollow hole formed in the pit of her stomach. Knowing the truth nearly paralyzed her.

Breathe, just breathe.

Wendy forced herself to focus. Yes, okay. Despite all her barriers and safeguards she'd gone ahead and fallen for the guy. Didn't mean she had to change her plans. She didn't have to tell him. Not until she had time to adjust to the idea. For now, she'd help Tom with Sam's new room, get as much finished as she could today, then head home. Originally, she'd planned to stay until Monday, but her nerves were on edge now and her composure was shot.

She got the coffee maker ready then pushed the button to start it. Her phone buzzed from the charging pad where Tom had put it for her last night, right beside his. Wendy turned it over to see her sister-in-law's number on the caller ID. She pushed the answer button.

"Hello?" Aiyana said. A baby screamed into the phone. "Wendy?"

"Hi. Everything okay over there?"

Burp! A belch worthy of a trucker came through the phone line.

"Oh, thank God!" Aiyana exclaimed. "That feels better."

"Was that you or the baby?"

"That was Kate. And now at least one of them is happy. Whew."

Wendy gave a tremulous smile, glad for the humor and a bit of stress relief. "I still can't believe you named them after royalty. William and Kate. Or that you now measure your life in burps."

"Also, milk letdowns and naps and puke-covered shoulders. Glamorous, right?"

Tears stung Wendy's eyes. All of that sounded pretty wonderful actually.

"How's Tom?" Aiyana asked.

"Fine," Wendy said, a little too quickly.

Her sister-in-law paused a moment. "What's wrong?"

"Nothing's wrong." She scowled. No way would she tell her sister-in-law about her birth control screwup or the fact she was in love. "I'm thinking maybe Tom and I should slow down a bit. Put some breathing space between us."

"But he's perfect for you!"

"He's not perfect for me. You don't even know him. Besides, he's a perfectionist and he's a single dad and—"

"And you're scared, aren't you? You always do this, Wendy. Why?"

"C'mon. It's Saturday and way too early for a lecture."

"Too bad."

The coffee maker beeped, and Wendy fixed herself a mug then sat on the comfy oversize sofa in the living room. "Look, I know it's only been a few weeks, but a lot has happened. Don't judge me."

"Then stop making excuses," her sister-in-law countered. "Please, Wendy. Live your life. Make the best of what you have."

"Stop." Wendy squeezed her eyes shut, letting her head flop back against the cushions. She rubbed her eyes, feeling exhausted despite having just gotten out of bed. "This whole thing is really hard."

"Does he know about the Huntington's?"

"He does."

"And he's still around." Her sister-in-law's smile came through in her tone. "Good man."

The knots in Wendy's gut tightened. "Tom *is* a really good guy, which is exactly why I should let him go. It's too risky. I'll only hurt him and his daughter more the longer I'm around."

A sigh echoed through the phone line. "Sweetie, I know you're terrified, but that's no reason to give up on what could be the best thing in your life."

"Maybe it is, though." Wendy scowled. "I'm not sure anymore."

"You have to find a way to push past it." Aiyana spoke slowly, her tone resigned. "Please don't use the possibility of HD to keep yourself from real love."

Damn. Her sister-in-law was right, even if Wendy was loath to admit it.

"We're redecorating his daughter's room this weekend while she's away. It's a surprise."

"You're staying at his place?"

The nervous tension inside Wendy pulled tighter. "Yes."

Another loud wail echoed through the phone line.

"Shoot. William's up again. Gotta go," Aiyana said. "We'll talk on Monday."

"Okay. I'll—"

Click.

Wendy groaned, letting the phone plop down on the sofa.

Not long afterward, the sound of a key grated in the front door lock. Wendy cracked her eyes open to see Tom, sweaty and carrying a takeout bag in one hand.

"Hey, you're up." He walked over to the breakfast bar. "I stopped and picked up food on the way home." He headed over to the sofa and bent to kiss her. "Let me shower and then we can eat."

She watched him disappear down the hallway toward the bedroom, her chest aching.

The sound of running water echoed from the rear of the apartment and Wendy pushed to her feet. Might as well make herself useful. She pulled the food from the bags then set out plates, silverware and napkins. Heavenly smells of roasted veggies and melted cheese wafted in the air. All this worrying had made her hungry. She started to peel open one of the foil wrappers to see what was inside, then yanked her hand away as Tom reentered the kitchen, dressed in a fresh white T-shirt and jeans, his hair still damp and his feet bare.

"Spinach, feta and egg white on whole wheat wraps." He gave her a quick hug. "Hope you like them."

"I'm sure I will." She settled on a stool and Tom pressed in close behind her, his hands on her hips and his mouth near her ear.

"How about a proper good-morning?" he whispered, his warm breath making her shiver.

She wanted to kiss him. Man, did she. But the

things she was grappling with inside her head were difficult enough, so she took a big bite of breakfast burrito instead. "Super-hungry."

"Hmm." Tom kissed her temple then took a seat beside her, unwrapping his breakfast.

They ate in silence for several minutes.

Speaking of being hungry, Wendy stared at her plate and willed away the images of them entwined together last night. Ugh. Those things wouldn't help her stick with her plan to bail early on this weekend. She shoved the rest of the delicious burrito into her mouth then stood to take her plate to the sink. After swallowing, she said, "Lots to do today. I'll meet you in Sam's bedroom."

She didn't wait for an answer, just hurried down the hall and got busy with a screwdriver, removing one of the two electrical outlet covers on the wall they'd be painting. Soon she sensed Tom's presence behind her, felt her body respond to him. Softening. Weakening. Accepting.

And while her rational self knew part of it had to be the intimacy of being here alone together in his apartment, she'd still been effectively and thoroughly seduced by his sweet words and loving touches. Mind and body. Heart and soul.

So much so that if she didn't skedaddle after they finished Sam's room today, she feared she wouldn't escape this weekend without irreparable damage to her heart. In fact, it was probably already too late.

"Did you learn your handyman skills from your dad and brothers too?" he asked.

She glanced back at him, happy to chat about her family and not think about the awkward conversation ahead. "Yep. I can also do roofing, plumbing and rebuild an engine in ten minutes flat."

She moved on to the next outlet, desperate to keep busy.

Tom got to work taping off the seam of an abutting wall. "Maybe I should call you by a superhero name instead of Wendy."

"Maybe you should." She gave him a quick wink. "I've been on my own a long time. Girl's got to take care of herself."

"What if you didn't, though," he said, not looking at her. "Have to be on your own, I mean. What if you had someone to help take care of you?"

She gathered up the outlet covers and screws, carried them to the closet, her hand shaking as she set them on top of a box, then picked up the other roll of painter's tape and moved a stepladder over to the wall before climbing to the top step. "I like not having to rely on anyone else."

He frowned. "You could, though. You could rely on me."

Truthfully, she'd love to have Tom to lean on, to confide in, to have and to hold. But it wasn't to be. She couldn't let it be. It wasn't fair to him or Sam. She'd applied about six inches of tape when Tom clamped his hands around her waist. She stopped, her heart tripping, and tilted her head down. "What are you doing?"

He looked up at her, gaze narrowed. "Figured this was easier than telling you to get down and let me do the ceiling."

"Probably."

"So I'm doing the next best thing by making sure you don't fall."

Wendy resumed her work, resorting to being snarky to cover the ache of affection in her chest. "You mean you're taking the opportunity to ogle my butt."

"Such a fine butt," he said with a satisfying amount of appreciation. "But I also meant what I said. I'm here for you, Wendy. Whenever and however you need me."

"Thanks." The word rasped out of her dry throat. She hated feeling trapped and right now everything seemed to be closing in rapidly around her. She quickly spread another foot or so of tape then climbed down to shift the stepladder. Tom kept his hands on her waist until she reached the floor. She stepped back and held the tape out to him. "If you want to do the ceiling, go ahead."

He smiled. "On further consideration, I'd rather be in charge of safety."

Rather than enjoy this flirty side of him far more than she should, Wendy moved the ladder and climbed back up to finish the job.

When she was done, Tom said, "Tell me more about your mom."

A topic she had no interest in discussing right now. "Why don't you turn on the radio instead? I like everything but rap."

"You still don't want to talk about her."

"Why the sudden interest?" She did her best not to sound defensive and failed, given his frown.

"Because I care about you, Wendy. A lot."

His confession swept the ground out from beneath her feet, leaving her in emotional free fall. Her elation over the fact he cared for her was quickly drowned by panic. Instead of being brave, she resorted to her old standby, avoidance. "Uh, how about those Anoraks? Think they'll make the playoffs this year? With Bobby Templeton back up to speed, they look pretty unbeatable."

"I'm trying to have a meaningful conversation here, Wendy," he said, his tone flat. "You know, the type consenting adults have when they care for one another."

"What's wrong with hockey?"

"Nothing's wrong with hockey. But I'd much rather know your feelings toward me."

Gah! The last thing she needed was for Tom to know how much she cared for him too. She couldn't tell him. Not until she'd made peace with it herself. It would only make it harder to go.

He'd stopped working and stood staring at her, his expression serious.

She sighed, grabbing a drop cloth to protect the floor, skirting the topic entirely once again by going back to his earlier question. "My mom was great. Funny, awesome in a crisis, and loved reading. She was my best friend, my confidante, my champion. Then she died, slowly and painfully. My dad and brothers did the best they could to raise me."

They'd done far more than their best. They were everything to her. Family was one of the most important tenets of Iñupiat life. And while she wasn't necessarily that tuned into her heritage in her daily life, she still kept that part alive and well. Seeing Tom and Sam grow closer together over the past few weeks had only reminded her how much she yearned for a family of her own. She turned away, blinking back tears. Crying wouldn't help. Her life was currently a big mess and she needed to clean it up. Starting with reinforcing those barriers around her heart before they crumbled completely, and it was too late.

Tom felt like an idiot. He hadn't meant to blurt out his feelings, but he wanted her to know she was important to him, that this wasn't just some fling, not in his eyes. Things had changed for him. He'd hoped they'd changed for her too.

Maybe this was a sign. Maybe his controlling tendencies were getting out of hand again. He'd known that bringing up the possibility of a long-term relationship with Wendy was risky, but damn. He was done avoiding the truth. Tom was ready to face facts.

Keeping his distance had been his plan, yet here he was, knee-deep in whatever this was with Wendy, and it felt like the tide was rising faster and faster. Her disease was a touchy subject for her. He got that. So were relationships, commitment. God knew, there were things he didn't like discussing either, but part of living meant dealing with things, so you could move on.

Frustrated, he rearranged the stack of tarps behind him.

He turned back to find Wendy on her hands and knees, taping the edge of a drop cloth to the floor. His chest squeezed tight. He loved Wendy. Deeply. Truly. And, yes, he wanted her. So badly it hurt. But he couldn't do this again. Not if she refused to be open and honest about her life and her disease. Yes, she was scared, but he had more than himself to think of now.

Sam had been through enough already with the death of her mother. He wouldn't put her through losing Wendy too. *Dammit.* If things weren't going to work out between them, he needed to know now, one way or another. That way they could make a clean break before Sam got back. And, yeah, maybe he was trying to control things again, trying to fit Wendy inside one of his neat little boxes when all she wanted was to be free.

Best to find out now. The longer he waited, the harder it would be.

Tom cleared his throat and forced himself to get back to work, taping a drop cloth into the corner. Wendy was beautiful, confident, smart, helpful, caring, fun, sexy, hardworking, dedicated. In fact, Tom couldn't think of one single thing he didn't like about her.

Except the fact she could be dying...

He didn't like that possibility at all.

Wendy pried off the lid of a paint can then turned it to face him. "Told you the shade was amazing. Sam's going to be thrilled."

"Spectacular," he said, looking at her and not the color.

Without comment she poured the paint into a roller pan.

Tom gathered up his brushes, opened both windows and they started to work. But as time dragged on, his niggle of unease grew. She'd never answered him about her feelings.

The silence closed in and the pressure to share…something, *anything*, built until he couldn't stand it any longer. "My mother went back to school to become a licensed clinical psychologist after I graduated med school," he said, concentrating on each thick, pink stroke. "I'm proud of her for doing it." He bent to get more paint on his brush. "Nothing like having your mom analyze your sex life at family dinners. Dad takes it all in his stride, of course. Retired Air Force guy. He's seen it all and wasn't impressed."

"They sound nice."

His parents were amazing, but anxiety was clawing inside him, urging him to get things settled here once and for all. Once Sam came home they'd be back to their regular schedules, their regular lives. Unless she allowed herself to open up with him, to be vulnerable like he was trying so hard to be with her, then those lives would have to be separate. They'd see each other at work. Wendy and Sam would still have their chats. His daughter would continue to volunteer in the Family Lounge in the ER, but it would be different.

There'd be no "them."

He wanted far more from Wendy than a fling, but he couldn't force her to get her test results or admit her feelings for him, just like he hadn't been able to force Nikki to stay in contact with him about their daughter or stop taking the drugs that had eventually killed her. Nope. It was Wendy's decision whether to get her results and all he could do was support her either way. It wasn't about him. And if she decided she didn't want him around anymore? Well, then, he'd have to find a way to be okay with it. Things between him and Sam had improved, with Wendy's help. They'd probably be okay now, even if his heart might not recover.

"Here's some trivia for your inquisitive mind." Wendy stopped painting and looked over at him. "When I was seven, my mom wanted to expose us to our cultural heritage, so she enrolled me and my brothers in Iñupiat language classes at the local library."

"That's cool. I'd love to learn your language someday."

She gave him a pointed stare then turned away to continue working.

Tom kept his mouth shut after that.

By late afternoon, the pink wall was done, much quicker than he'd anticipated. They still had to let it dry before putting up the shelves and pictures and moving the furniture back into place, but the time had come for some serious talk and answers. He glanced at the clock. Six p.m. "Uh, want to take a walk before dinner?"

Wendy set her roller aside and wiped her

hands on her scrub pants, her expression oddly somber. "A walk sounds great. The sunset should be beautiful tonight."

CHAPTER THIRTEEN

WENDY CHANGED INTO jeans and an Anchorage Mercy T-shirt, then went outside to wait for Tom on the sidewalk. The sun was low enough in the sky to cast long shadows and the breeze blowing in off the inlet was cool enough to take the edge off the heat. The temperatures had been unusually warm the past week. She tapped the toe of her flip-flop on the cement, feeling edgy and nervous about the conversation ahead.

He stepped outside a few minutes later, still wearing the same clothes but with sneakers. He slid an arm around her waist and she buried her face in his shoulder and inhaled his good smell. Tom pulled back to kiss her.

Wendy looped her arm through his, leading him down the sidewalk toward Tikishla Park.

He squeezed her closer into his side. "Listen, about earlier…"

Dread clawed through her as they strolled down East Northern Light Boulevard and dusk settled in. No baseball games tonight, it appeared. The Little League ball diamond was dark. Seemed symbolic somehow. They stopped at the corner and he took her hand. "I know you're afraid, Wendy. I am too. But I love you. Please don't push me away. We can get through this if you let me in and share with me what you're feeling."

Her blood pounded so hard in her ears it drowned out everything else.

Tell him. Get out now, before you can't.

They walked on a bit farther. The silence between them grew taut.

The white of his T-shirt faded to light gray as the moon peeked out from behind a cloud. Tom looked ethereal, the ends of his blond hair glowing slightly.

They walked on into the park and took a seat on a wooden bench to watch the sunset. Vibrant pinks, purples and golds streaked the sky. Tom put his arm around her shoulders again, pulling her closer, making her yearn for all the things she'd never allowed herself to have. The temperature dropped as twilight descended and he whispered in her ear, "Tell me what you're thinking."

Wendy closed her eyes and forced herself to scoot away from him. "I'm thinking this isn't a good idea, Tom. Being around you has me confused and distracted and I need time to figure all this out." Her stomach lurched, the words slicing like raw glass in her throat. She squeezed her eyes shut and made herself continue. "This weekend was great and all, but I never wanted a relationship. I told you that from the start. You said you loved me but I'm a loner. You want honesty? We had a nice couple of nights together. Time to end on a high note."

He pulled back slightly, deep lines forming between his brows as his frown deepened. "Wait a minute, Wendy. This is more than just sex. I feel it and I think you do too." When she didn't respond, he pulled away too, scowling. "You're doing it again. Shutting me out. Dammit." He raked a hand through his hair while she stared at her toes. "What about Sam?"

"What about her? Like you said, she and I can continue to meet for our chats. She never has to know about any of this." If she stayed one more second, she'd end up telling him everything—all her fears, all her dreams, all her feelings for him and for Sam. Energy ricocheted inside her like a pinball. She had to go, had to run. Now. Before it was too late. Wendy stood, hugging her arms around her middle to keep from reaching for him. "Trust me. This is for the best. Let's just keep things light. Nothing has to change."

"Things damn well do have to change, Wendy. I just told you that I loved you." Tom pushed to his feet, anger and hurt shining in his blue eyes. "Doesn't that mean anything? How the hell can you stand there and tell me what's best for me and Sam when you don't even have the courage to face your own fears? People call me a control freak, but you're the one with the complex here. You think if you ignore what scares you, you'll be safe, but life doesn't work that way. I've told you how I feel, what I want. I've tried to show you I'll be there for you, tried to hold on, but I'm done. I won't repeat the same mistakes I did with Nikki."

He pinched the bridge of his nose. "This time I'm taking the hint."

She blanched, tears welling. "I'm sorry but whatever this is, I can't handle it right now."

"Goodbye, Wendy." With that, he turned and walked away, heading back toward his apartment, leaving her there alone with too many feelings, too much regret, only to have a little corgi come around the corner and sniff her feet.

"Oh, hey." A college kid wearing an Anchorage Anoraks hockey jersey followed, pulling on the dog's leash. "C'mon, Daisy." The kid tugged the dog away. "She thinks everyone's here to see her. Have a good night."

Wendy headed back toward home as well, the knot in her gut tightening as she spotted Tom up ahead. He'd stopped to pick at a loose thread at the hem of his shirt, his stress habit on full display again.

The tension inside her that had been building since that morning boiled over into anger. She had a right to be controlling about her life, her future, dammit. He had no right to an opinion on her choices. None at all. He might want the last say here, but she didn't have to give it to him.

"So that's it, then?" she yelled as she drew closer to him, knowing she should walk away but unable to leave him. Not yet. "You say it's over and, boom, we're done? Great. Perfect. That's pretty damned controlling, Tom."

"Why do you care?" He backed away, nearing the curb. "You're a loner, remember? You said you wanted no strings, no commitment. Well, here you go. No, wait." He snapped his fingers and made a show of having an epiphany. "Once again, I'm handing you exactly what you say you want on a silver platter and what are you doing? Pushing me away. What a shocker!"

"Fine. You're right. I'm damaged. I'm broken. I'm shoving you away." She sniffled and brushed her hand across her damp cheek. "But I'm also not yours to fix!"

"I don't want to fix you, Wendy," he said, throwing up his hands in a sign of surrender. "I just wanted to love you. That's it. Sorry that doesn't fit in with your plans."

He started across the street, not looking both ways and not looking back either.

Wendy covered her face with her hands. She should let him go. This was what she'd wanted. To be alone. He was right. Right about everything. She had pushed him away…she was avoiding her fears. And if she went after him all her defenses would vanish, and she'd be right back where she'd started.

She couldn't do it. Wouldn't do it. No matter how her heart was screaming in agony.

Then a hideous screech of tires ripped through the air, followed by a sickening thud.

Wendy lowered her hands to see Tom lying in the street, his motionless body highlighted by the twin beams of a vehicle's headlamps. She took off running toward the accident scene, her heart in her throat. "No!"

Sprawled on the warm pavement, blinking up at the starry sky, stunned, Tom couldn't help wondering when in hell his universe had imploded. He'd been so careful his entire life, following every rule, never straying, being better than the best, proving himself over and over, because he was, after all, the son of an Air Force drill sergeant.

Mind the job, bub.

He'd certainly minded it well this time, hadn't he? Even when he'd tried not to control everything, he'd still managed to make a mess of it all. Somehow what should have been a fun, carefree weekend with Wendy had gone very wrong. The defensiveness that had made him so righteously indignant and had triggered his anger during their argument now deflated.

Why was he in the road? He remembered walking away, because he refused to go down the same path he had with his ex-wife. He wouldn't be the one holding on again when all hope was lost, just because of his stupid phobias and fears.

Wendy had taught him to let go. He loved her enough to set her free, if that's what made her happy. Then…

Bam!

A loud noise.

A hard smack on his left side and the sensation of flying.

His head pounded, and the incessant smell of gasoline and the sound of an engine nearby drowned out the comforting sound of crickets. He tried to raise his left arm, but it didn't seem to work.

Pain seared along his nerve endings as his memory returned. His pulse raced as adrenaline flooded his system. Sirens wailed in the distance, growing closer by the second. He'd been hit by a car. Him. Mr. Careful. Mr. Always-Look-Twice-Before-You-Leap.

His left shoulder and hip ached too, and his left cheekbone was killing him.

"Tom!" Wendy's voice washed over him like a balm as she knelt by his side. "Oh, God. Don't move. Help is on the way. Stay with me." Her gentle words and sweet fragrance lingered as darkness encroached. "Please stay with me. Please don't leave me."

"I didn't see him, I swear," an unknown voice said, echoing inside his head. "He walked right out in front of my car without even looking."

Please don't leave me...

If Tom hadn't been in so much agony he would've laughed. She'd finally admitted she needed him around at least, and all it had taken was a near-death experience. They were making progress.

His last conscious thoughts were of Wendy and Sam, before the pain turned to oblivion and blissful nothingness overtook him.

CHAPTER FOURTEEN

WENDY RUSHED INTO Anchorage Mercy ER alongside the gurney. Zac was once again the paramedic on duty and wheeled Tom in. Jake met them at the ambulance entrance. It was weird being on this side of the situation again. Weird and way more stressful than the twins' delivery had been. Because this time Tom was in danger.

Jake met Wendy's gaze for a moment before turning to Zac. "Give me the rundown."

"Thirty-four-year-old male with loss of consciousness after being struck by a motor vehicle. Contusions on the left shoulder and hip and a two-centimeter laceration on the left cheekbone." Zac's voice was calm and clear, even as he gave Wendy a sympathetic look. The ER crew took over and steered Tom's gurney into Trauma Bay Three.

Zac clapped Wendy on the shoulder once the

curtains were closed on Tom's area, shutting them out in the hallway. "I'm sure he'll be fine. Don't worry, okay? I've seen a lot of these accidents over the years and it's not as bad as it looks. He's young and strong and healthy. Call me if you need anything, okay?"

She swallowed hard and gave him a curt nod, but not worrying was out of the question.

Zac headed back outside to check on his rig and Wendy stood just beyond the curtain of Tom's area, uncertain what to do. The nurse in her wanted to charge inside and make sure he was treated properly. The woman in her was petrified of losing another person she loved.

Yep. She loved Tom Farber. So much her heart felt ready to burst with it. Figured she could admit it now, when it might just be too late.

Please, God, don't let it be too late.

Thankfully, as usual, Jake talked his way through the exam, keeping her apprised of Tom's condition. "Two pulse radials bilaterally. No fractures noted on palpation, but we'll need to get X-rays on all extremities and C-spine for fractures, and an MRI of that left shoulder and his head. I'm suspecting a dislocation. Contusions on left shoulder and hip. Checking inside his mouth. No broken teeth or injuries. Airways clear and breathing normal. Pupils are equal and reactive to light. Let's get him to MRI and see what's going on inside his skull, check for possible concussion and rule out intracranial bleeding. Order an ultrasound too to check for any abdominal injuries. Tom? Dr. Thomas Farber, can you hear me?"

Wendy held her breath, hoping to hear Tom's voice. But nothing.

"Tom?" Jake tried again. "Nope. He's still out. Localizes to pain on all extremities. Good. Okay, people. Let's get him out of here and up to MRI now, please."

The curtain swooshed aside, and Jake strode over to where Wendy leaned against the wall because she was afraid her legs wouldn't support her. He took off his gloves and gown then guided her into a small private waiting room nearby. Once the door closed behind them, he pulled her into a hug, rubbing her stiff back. "He's good, Wen. Well, as good as you can be after getting hit by a car. I'm sending him for an MRI to see if there's a concussion, but otherwise he's okay. We'll get X-rays to make sure nothing's broken, and he'll probably be sore for a couple of weeks, maybe a sling if that shoulder's dislocated, but he should heal fine. What happened?"

All the fear and the pain and the emotions Wendy had kept bottled up for so long came pouring out in one long rush of a sentence. "I spent the weekend with Tom and we were re-decorating his daughter's room as a surprise for her when she got home and I got scared because I love Tom but I shouldn't because I'm not good for him with my medical history and Sam needs a new mom but I could be dying and I think I've messed up everything good in my life because I'm too frightened to face the truth and…"

Her words trailed off and her vision dissolved in tears.

Jake patiently took all that in, frowning as he gently pushed Wendy into a seat then took the chair beside hers, holding her until her sobbing eased. Then he sat back and took her hands. "Right. Good. Feeling better?"

She nodded, feeling oddly numb after pouring out all those long-suppressed secrets and feelings.

"Okay. I'm glad to hear you're in love. Finally." He kept hold of her hands, warming her icy fingers. "As someone who has some experience at messing up the best things in his life, I can tell you you'll get through this. Impossible as it seems right now, you will. If you stay open and don't give up on each other."

Wendy exhaled, sniffling. "Tom will be okay?"

"I think so, yes. Of course, I'll have to wait for all the results to be sure but, yeah. I think he'll make a full recovery. We'll probably keep him overnight for observation, to be on the safe side."

"Thanks, buddy." She hugged Jake again then sat back, grabbing a tissue from the box on the table beside her. "I've decided I'm going to call on Tuesday and get my test results."

"Wow." Jake watched her closely. "What brought on this decision?"

She cringed. "Right before the accident, Tom broke up with me. He said I was letting my fears control my life. That I was being controlling." Her ironic chuckle came out weak and raspy because of the crying she'd done. "Which is funny because this whole time that's what he's been trying to avoid doing with me because of his ex-wife."

At Jake's confused expression, she gave a dismissive wave. "Anyway, he's right. That's exactly my problem. Avoiding life, avoiding my test results, avoiding love, because I thought if I pretended they weren't there or weren't important to me then I wouldn't get hurt." She shook her head.

"But I got hurt anyway, because I ended up pushing away the best things in my life. So I'm done. I'm getting my tests results because it's time to know the truth. Because I want what you and Molly have. Because I want a life and love and babies and a future with Tom that doesn't involve a million cats, like you said."

"Wow." Jake leaned back in his chair. "I'll be here for you, no matter what. You know that, right?"

"I do." She smiled through her tears. "Thanks. I mean, I know it's a long shot, given that all my brothers are negative." She sighed. "But I'm still praying I'm mutation-free too."

A nurse knocked then stuck her head into the room. "Uh, Jake, we need another doc on the floor. Got a new GSW en route. Also, the cops are here to talk to Wendy about the accident."

"Great. Another gunshot wound. On my way." Jake rubbed his eyes before pushing to his feet, stopping at the door and turning back to Wendy, handing her a plastic bag containing Tom's clothes and his personal effects. "I'll tell the cops you're in here if you're ready to give your report. Take as long as you need. Make yourself comfortable. I'll let you know about Tom as soon as I hear something."

"Thanks." While she waited for the police, Wendy pulled Tom's cellphone from the bag and scrolled through his contacts, looking for his parents' number. They were due to bring Sam home on Monday, but they needed to know what was going on. Tom looked like he'd gone six rounds with Rocky Balboa at the moment, regardless if there was any permanent damage or not. After everything Sam had been through, the last thing the kid needed was to arrive home unprepared to see her dad post-accident.

Fresh nerves washed over Wendy as she dialed the number then waited for someone to pick up the line.

Finally, on the third ring, a woman answered. "Hello? Farber residence."

"Uh, hi. You don't know me, but my name's Wendy Smith and I work with your son, Tom, at the hospital in Anchorage." She hadn't felt this shaky since she'd called the house of the first boy she'd liked back in fifth grade. "I'm calling to let you know your son—"

"Oh, my gosh. You're *that* Wendy, aren't you?" his mother said. "Sam's told us so much about you. She's really taken with you. How nice to finally speak with you."

Warmth spread from Wendy's chest outward, unexpected but not unpleasant. For once, hearing that someone might care for her too didn't make her feel like running away. If anything, it made her want to run upstairs to the MRI room and be with Tom. First things first, though.

"Thank you. It's nice to speak with you too," Wendy said, before switching into nurse mode.

"Listen, there's been a bit of an accident. Please don't be alarmed, but your son was struck by a car tonight."

"Good Lord!" There was rustling as Tom's mother relayed the information to his father then came back on the line. "Is Tommy all right?"

"The doctor thinks he'll be fine, but he might have a concussion and possibly a dislocated shoulder. They want to keep him overnight here at Anchorage Mercy for observation. I didn't want to upset Sam but thought I should let you know before you bring her home. The poor kid's been through enough."

"Oh, thank goodness our son's all right," his mother said. "And no. We don't want to upset Sam. She's been having a great time here with us. Should we head back tonight? Sam's sleeping, but we can wake her if you think it's necessary."

"No, no. Let her sleep." Wendy looked up as Jake stuck his head back into the waiting room. Two uniformed police officers stood behind him. Time to go. "Just maybe explain it to her tomorrow. Pending the MRI and X-rays,

Tom shouldn't have any lasting damage, but he's pretty bruised and he has a cut on his left cheek. You can bring her home as scheduled on Monday and all should be good."

"Hmm. We'll see after we tell her tomorrow," his mother said. "Please call us if anything changes. And I'll look forward to meeting you in person."

Wendy ended the call then signaled for the cops to come in. The interview went pretty quickly, seeing that she'd not really observed the accident at all. They finished up by asking her if Tom planned to press charges. She told them she didn't think so, but they could ask him tomorrow. This day had ended badly enough for all of them. The driver was a woman in her sixties who'd been as traumatized by seeing Tom lying in the road as Wendy had been. Best to put this behind them and start afresh, at least in her opinion.

The officers left, and Wendy wandered back out into the controlled chaos of the ER. Jake was in between patients, writing out prescriptions at the nurses' station. He waved Wendy over.

"Good news. The MRI and X-rays were negative. No bleeding in his brain, nothing broken. But he did suffer an acute anterior dislocation of his left shoulder. We set it at thirty degrees external rotation and he'll need to wear a sling on that arm for three weeks, then see the ortho doc for a recheck."

Wendy sagged with relief. "Thank God. Are you still keeping him overnight?"

"Yeah, he's still out of it. Poor guy." Jake walked around the desk to look up the number. "He'll be up on the fifth floor. Room 506."

"Thanks. And tell Zac thanks for all his help too, if you see him again." Wendy headed for the elevators. For the first time in a long time she felt like she was getting a second chance and she wasn't about to let it slip away. "I'll be in Tom's room if you need me."

Tom blinked his eyes open to bright light streaming in through the windows and an annoying bleeping noise coming from somewhere nearby. His whole body ached, and there was a weird pulling on his left cheek. He went to brush it away with his left hand, but a throbbing pain in that shoulder stopped him. He frowned and yawned then turned his head slightly to see an array of monitors beside him with wires attached to his right arm and chest.

Hospital. He was in the hospital. Why?

His head hurt, but he forced himself to think. Right. He'd broken up with Wendy last night. Well, not really, since they'd never officially been a couple. At least not to her. To him? He'd have loved to call her his own.

My Wendy.

He turned slightly in the other direction to see her curled up in a chair beside his bed, sound asleep, one hand holding his, warm and steady. She had a book clutched to her chest. *Little Women.* The automatic blood-pressure cuff on his arm inflated again, pinching his skin. They'd been in the park. They'd argued. That's when he'd walked out into the street.

Idiot.

She was here, but that didn't mean all was forgiven. If she didn't want him, he wouldn't—couldn't—be *that guy.* Indecision and resignation, along with his throbbing temples, made him wince.

At the same time, he still yearned to be with

her. He wanted to apologize for the things he'd said, for trying to control the uncontrollable, though he'd never apologize for loving her. He wanted to go for more walks, to drink more coffees, to have more dinners, to explore Anchorage with her and Sam and have fun. To have not-fun too—like cleaning or laundry or more decorating and painting pink walls. To spend more time with her and Sam together, as a family. Do all the silly, simple things that everyone took for granted.

More than anything, he wanted to thank Wendy for helping him get his daughter back.

But given how they'd ended things, Tom doubted that was even possible.

He wiggled his toes to make sure they still worked and felt a zinging pain through his left hip. Teeth gritted, he tried to scoot up in bed, the coursing pain in his body making his eyes water. He must have landed on his left side after the car had hit him because that half of him felt like a solid chunk of agony.

"Tom?" Wendy stirred, her husky whisper stopping him cold.

She blinked at him, her gaze unfocused.

"Have you been here all night?" he asked, his throat dry and his cheek stinging.

"Of course." She straightened and set her book aside. "How do you feel?"

"Like I got run over by a Mack truck."

"More like a Prius." She smiled, and his world brightened. "I'm so glad you're okay."

"Me too." He tried to move again, but the pain stopped him. "Did you tell Sam? I don't want her to worry about me."

"I called your parents last night and told them what happened. They're going to tell her today." She bit her lip and cringed. "I hope that's okay. I thought they should know."

He tried to smile, but his cheek made it hard. "Thanks. Looks like Mom's psychology degree will come in handy after all, eh?"

"Yeah." She tucked her hair behind her ear and stared down at her toes. "And you don't need to thank me. In fact, I owe you an apology for last night. I wasn't thinking clearly, and I panicked, and you paid the price. I'll never forgive myself for you getting hurt because of me."

The catch in her voice was too much for him

to bear. Tom tugged on her hand, drawing her closer. "What happened last night wasn't your fault, Wendy. You had no way of knowing this would happen. None. We're both dealing with stuff. It's okay."

"It's not okay." She shook her head, causing her hair to fall across her face again. He longed to push it away, but she had hold of his good hand, so instead he sighed. And listened. "You were right. I have been letting my fear control me, but I'm done. I'm going to call and get my test results. On Tuesday. Right after the holiday."

"Wendy, are you sure?"

"I am. Because of you." She shrugged and bit her lip. "Thanks to you, I'm summoning my courage and finding out. I've put this off long enough and if I'm going to become more involved in your life and Sam's, then I need to know I can be there for you both."

Tom nodded, regretting the move instantly as the room spun dizzily.

"I love you, Tom Farber," Wendy said, her voice rough with emotion. "I'd like to be with you, for whatever time I have left—days, years, whatever."

He took that in for a minute. "Are you saying you want to date me?"

She gave him an irritated stare. "I'm saying I'm committed to you, you stubborn man. I'm committed to whatever the future holds for us. I love you. I wanted you to know. I'm tired of living with secrets."

Tom couldn't contain his grin this time, no matter how badly his cheek throbbed. "Agreed. No more secrets. I love you too, Wendy Smith. And I promise I'll do my best not to be as stubborn or controlling or rule-abiding anymore."

Wendy leaned in to place a gentle kiss on his lips. "Now we just have to run it by Sam to get her approval."

As if on cue, a knock sounded at the door to his private hospital room and in trundled Tom's parents with his daughter. Sam's face was red and splotchy from crying and her expression was distraught. Before the door had even closed she rushed to Tom's hospital bed and practically hurled herself on his chest, hugging him and kissing him. It hurt like hell, to be honest, but he wouldn't have changed it for the world. "Oh, my God. When Grandma and Grandpa told me what happened, I made them drive me home. Please don't die on me, Dad. Please!"

Tom let go of Wendy's hand to hold his daughter close to his heart, like he'd wanted to since the moment she'd entered his life. He kissed the top of her head, inhaling the fragrance of the floral shampoo she liked. "I'm fine, sweetie. I'm not dying. Well, not for a long time anyway. I had a little accident last night, but they tell me I'll make a full recovery. Right, Wendy?"

He glanced over at her beside his bed and found her swiping away tears as well. His heart ached with so much love for both of these fantastic women in his life.

"Yep. Your dad's going to be fine, Sam." Wendy sniffled. "He's too bullheaded to die."

Tom's mother raised an eyebrow. "Got that right. Our Tommy was always getting himself into scrapes when he was younger. Too inquisitive for his own good." She walked around the bed to hug Wendy. "Alice Farber, by the way."

"You look like hell, son," his dad said, carefully patting Tom's uninjured right shoulder. "Glad you're okay."

"Me too, Dad." Tom couldn't seem to stop smiling now. "Me too."

His mom let Wendy go and kissed her son's forehead before walking back over to stand beside his dad. "What's the golden rule here?"

"Look before you cross?" Tom's sarcasm earned him a snort from Wendy and a flat stare from his mother. "What?"

"Treasure the ones you love," his mom said, in her best psychologist tone.

"Dad?" Sam straightened and wiped her eyes. "I'm sorry for the way I acted before. I was just so sad about Mom and scared you'd go away and leave me too. I love you."

Tom's heart felt like it would burst. "I love you too, sweetie. So much."

"We have a surprise for you, Sam." Wendy moved in beside Tom and took his hand again. "Back at your apartment."

"A surprise?" Sam's eyes widened. "Really?"

"I hope you like it. We worked hard to redo your room this weekend."

"Yes! I can't wait to see it!" A delighted

squeal issued from the twelve-year-old before her gaze dropped to Tom's and Wendy's joined hands. "Wait. Are you guys together now? I *knew* you liked each other."

Tom glanced over at Wendy, all pain forgotten under the rush of sweetness in his system. "Yeah, I plan on keeping Wendy around as long as she'll have me."

"For better or worse?" Wendy asked, taking a seat on the edge of his bed.

"For always." He brought her hand to his lips for a kiss.

She smiled, then leaned closer. "Like I told your daughter, I don't usually like that word. *Always.* But in this case, I'll make an exception because it's true."

CHAPTER FIFTEEN

Six months later...

"Do you see the server anywhere?" Wendy asked Tom, who was sitting beside her at their large round table for fourteen at the Snaggle Tooth. Friday night meant the pub was packed and between the white noise of conversation and the sounds of cooking food and drinks being served it was a bit hard to hear. "I need a refill on my water."

"Anything for you, *asik*," Tom said, kissing her temple.

Sam, who was sitting on Wendy's other side, wrinkled her nose. "*Ew*. No PDAs."

"What's wrong with public displays of affection?" Wendy asked, snagging a fry from Sam's plate. She was eating for two now. That was her excuse anyway. *Asik* was a term of endearment in Iñupiat. Tom called her his dear one and he was her *avu*—her sugar.

Sam soon lost interest and instead focused on the friend she'd brought along, who was also spending the night at their house. She'd turned thirteen a month ago and so far, so good. After Tom's short stint in the hospital back over Memorial Day weekend, their relationship had improved steadily. Sam and her father were finally opening up to each other and building a lasting bond.

Wendy and Tom's relationship was moving right along too. They'd bought a house together after their leases were up. Things were good. Her life was a miracle if she'd ever seen one, but everything lately had seemed blessed beyond belief. Especially since her test results had come back negative for Huntington's disease.

She'd actually not called that Tuesday. They'd waited until she could sit down with Sam one night and tell her about the disease and prepare her in case things didn't go well. It had been hard, after all those years of not knowing, to find out the answer at last. Harder still had been watching Sam go through the same uncertainty and fears that Wendy had had herself with her mom, but Tom had been by her side every step of the way, his quiet support and gentle strength everything to her.

And when she'd made that fateful phone call and found out she was negative, she'd swear Tom's shouts of joy could've been heard all the way across the Bering Straits into Russia and Sam's high-pitched squeals of delight probably called to all the humpbacks currently swimming in Cook Inlet.

Afterward, they'd gone out as a family to celebrate, right here at the Snaggle Tooth. No more table for one, no more feeling like she was standing on the outside, looking in at the world everyone else inhabited. She was a part of it all now, thanks to Tom. He'd given her the courage to overcome her fears and face the future. She'd given him back his daughter.

And now they were having a child together. Such a lovely, unexpected surprise. She'd never expected to have a baby of her own and now she couldn't imagine a world without a kid with her dark hair and Tom's lovely blue eyes. Or his blond hair and her dark eyes. Either way, the child would be loved and spoiled to within an inch of its precious little life.

Even Sam was digging her new role as big sister, helping Wendy pick out furniture for the nursery and offering to babysit whenever they needed her. Her grades had improved at school and she was now on the honor roll. And she'd continued reading in the family lounge and had even volunteered to help other at-risk kids by sitting in on a new group the counselor had started once a week at the hospital.

Things had come full circle and Wendy felt more and more blessed each day.

"Refill on your water, ma'am," the waiter said, setting a fresh glass down in front of her. It was the same guy who'd served her and Aiyana back in May, the day her sister-in-law had gone into labor. "Anything else I can get you right now?"

"I'm good, thanks."

Tom was everything she'd wanted in a partner. And, yeah, he wasn't perfect. He still got stressed and overly persnickety sometimes, but she was quick to put him in his place. They balanced each other out, since he called her out on her avoidance issues when things got too emotional. They were a great match, *nungu-suitok*—eternal. Tom had even taken an Iñupiat language refresher course with her, for when their baby came. Wendy appreciated his efforts, even if he fumbled the words most of the time. She found his mistakes endearing.

True love indeed.

"Have you picked out names yet?" Aiyana asked from across the table. She and Ned were having a rare night away from the twins. They were enjoying all the alone time they could, since Aiyana had just found out she was pregnant again too. She patted her own belly. "We're thinking Harry, of course, whether it's a boy or a girl."

"Well, since *we're* definitely having a girl," Wendy said, "we're going with Beatrice Alice, after our moms. We can call her Trixie for short."

"Or not," Tom added, chuckling as he snuggled Wendy closer into his side. "I like Bibi better as a nickname."

"You also like haggis and the Patriots. I don't really think you get a say, *avu*." She kissed him quickly then laughed. She liked the little moments of intimacy among the chaos of preparing for their upcoming wedding along with the birth in a little over three months.

Time had certainly flown.

Speaking of the birth, her midwife, Carmen, was at the dinner too, along with Zac Taylor. Wendy had always suspected there was more than friendship brewing between those two, but both denied any such thing. As she devoured another buffalo barbecue chicken tender, Wendy watched them banter and flirt with the best of them.

Yep. All those two needed was the right push and they'd tumble into love just fine.

Jake and Molly were there too, along with Wendy's other two brothers, Jim and Mike, and their long-time girlfriends. Maybe the Snaggle Tooth would work its magic on them as well.

She hoped so. Turned out love was pretty darned grand after all.

Wendy traced her fingers over the slight scar on Tom's left cheek from the accident, wanting to hold this moment inside and never let it go. To think she'd lived for years trying to shut all this out, all the love and the pain and the glory, thinking she was protecting herself, but instead she'd just been missing out. She'd almost lost the man she loved before she'd ever really had him.

"What, *asik*?" Tom looked down at her with such tenderness it took her breath away. He caught her hand and kissed her fingers, his expression concerned. "Everything okay?"

"Everything's wonderful." She smiled, tears in her eyes, and not because of her wacky hormones either. Jake teased her these days, saying she was getting sappy on him, but the truth was she felt filled to bursting with gratefulness. "Thank you."

"For what?" he asked, the sounds around them fading as they focused on each other.

"For loving me when I thought I was too screwed up to be with someone normal."

"If I'm normal, then the world's in trouble," he said quietly. "But now you have me, Wendy. The same way I'm there for you. We're a team, you and me and Sam. And our baby, once she arrives."

She leaned closer. He did too.

He buried his face in her hair and she breathed in his good Tom smell.

Things weren't perfect. But they were right.

And that was all Wendy ever wanted.

Sam and her friend stood. "Is it okay if we go over and play video games?"

"Stay where I can see you," Tom said.

His daughter gave him a quick kiss and a hug, before running off with her friend to the opposite corner of the pub where the other kids their age were hanging out.

Tom looked down at Wendy again. "What are you thinking? You're awfully quiet."

"Honestly?" She looked up at him. He nodded. "I'm thinking I love you and I want you around for a long, long time."

The baby took that opportunity to kick hard against Wendy's ribs. She winced then brought Tom's free hand down to her belly, so he could feel their little gymnast flipping around inside her. Another dream she'd almost given up on because of her fear. She closed her eyes and said a silent prayer of thanks for all this joy, then looked around the table at all their family and friends who'd be there for them and Sam and their baby. They were so, so lucky.

Miracles truly were all around them.

"Define a long time," he said, nuzzling her temple, his hand warm and strong on her baby bump as he brought her back to the present moment.

"How about forever?" Wendy kissed him.

"Forever sounds perfect to me," Tom murmured against her lips.

* * * * *

LET'S TALK
Romance

For exclusive extracts, competitions
and special offers, find us online:

- facebook.com/millsandboon
- @millsandboonuk
- @millsandboon

Or get in touch on 0844 844 1351*

For all the latest titles coming soon,
visit millsandboon.co.uk/nextmonth

Want even more
ROMANCE?

Join our bookclub today!

'Mills & Boon books, the perfect way to escape for an hour or so.'

Miss W. Dyer

'Excellent service, promptly delivered and very good subscription choices.'

Miss A. Pearson

'You get fantastic special offers and the chance to get books before they hit the shops'

Mrs V. Hall

Visit millsandbook.co.uk/Bookclub and save on brand new books.

MILLS & BOON